DEATH IN SILHOUETTE

Maria Black, headmistress-detective, is invited to the engagement celebrations of an ex-pupil — and becomes involved in the apparent suicide of the prospective bridegroom, Keith Robinson. The circumstances — death by hanging in a locked cellar — satisfy the coroner that Robinson took his own life. However, 'Black Maria' thinks otherwise, and sets out, with her companion 'Pulp' Martin, to prove how Keith really died. She uncovers a plan of cold-blooded murder. But who is the killer — and why was Robinson killed?

JOHN RUSSELL FEARN

DEATH IN SILHOUETTE

Complete and Unabridged

LINFORD
Leicester

First published in Great Britain

First Linford Edition
published 2007

British Library CIP Data

Fearn, John Russell, *1908 – 1960*
Death in silhouette.—Large print ed.—
Linford mystery library
1. School principals—Fiction 2. Murder
—Investigation—Fiction 3. Detective and
mystery stories 4. Large type books
I. Title II. Slate, John, *1908 – 1960*
823.9'12 [F]

ISBN 978–1–84617–790–3

Published by
F. A. Thorpe (Publishing)
Anstey, Leicestershire

Set by Words & Graphics Ltd.
Anstey, Leicestershire
Printed and bound in Great Britain by
T. J. International Ltd., Padstow, Cornwall

This book is printed on acid-free paper

1

For the past ten minutes Patricia Taylor had been watching either the big clock on the wall of the restaurant, or the wide glass doors of the entrance way.

As the clock hands passed six o'clock two things happened. A slightly built young man went past the glass doors outside and raised a hand in a brief signal. Behind Patricia roly-poly Madge Banning stood ready to take over. For Pat the day's work was finished.

'Your boy friend just went past,' Madge Banning said, and nodded her blonde head towards the doors.

'As if I didn't know!' Pat made a grab at her hat.

'Don't know why you don't make a go of it,' Madge sighed. 'I know what *I'd* do if I had a handsome guy like him to give a tumble . . . ' Madge sighed as amorous thoughts floated through her none-too-brilliant brain.

'I'll invite you to the wedding — if any,' Pat smiled. 'See you tomorrow.'

'If I'm alive,' Madge agreed, who lived only for today.

Pat hurried towards the doors, clutching her handbag as though she were about to start a relay race.

Outside the air was no cooler than in the restaurant, though mercifully devoid of the ever-present smell of cooking. Redford, in Essex, was a small town and in the summer managed to maintain the record for being stiflingly hot. The torrid sun beat down on Pat as she glanced along the busy street.

Three shops farther away Keith Robinson turned and came swiftly in her direction.

'Hello there, Pat!' He gave one of his rare smiles. 'One thing about disliking your work: it makes you hurry out on time so you can meet me.'

'I would do that anyway,' Pat said. 'And what's the surprise you mentioned in your letter?' She jerked the handbag under her arm to emphasize that the letter was within it. 'You've got me all excited.'

'Good!' he approved. 'That was why I sent it . . . '

They began a leisurely walk along the street. Two streams of people were flowing past — one leaving work and the other coming into town for the evening's pleasures, most of which were condensed into this main street. The business quarters, where Pat's father and brother worked — an engineer and solicitor's clerk respectively — were on the outskirts, beyond which again lay the suburbs.

As they walked, pride kept Pat from asking again about the surprise. Instead she changed the subject.

'I've been thinking, Keith,' she said. 'We take this walk home every working day, and at weekends we just take a longer walk. I mean, as it stands there isn't much future in it, is there?'

'Isn't much future in anything if it comes to that,' he told her, and his mood had abruptly changed to deepest gloom.

Pat sighed. This was one thing about Keith Robinson that she had always found difficult to tolerate — his queer changes of mood without any apparent reason; and at times his studied refusal to answer simple questions. It was as though he occasionally shut up inside himself and became oblivious to the outer world. However, no man can be perfect, so she was prepared to make allowances. After all, he *was* handsome. He was a costings clerk at the main railway goods station. Perhaps figures could make one behave queerly . . .

'We can settle it, of course!' Keith said suddenly, as they turned a corner.

'Settle what?' Pat came out of her thoughts with a start.

'About us. I agree there isn't any point in just walking about. It's a build-up, really. That,' he added, with an odd little smile, 'is the surprise I mentioned. I'm not much good at talking — So here!' he broke off, digging into his jacket. 'This'll explain better than I can!'

A small, square, leather-surfaced box lay in the centre of his slender palm. Pat gazed at it in fascination. Keith's finger and thumb snapped open the box lid. The bright evening sun set a three-stone diamond ring glittering.

'Why, Keith, it's — '

Pat stopped as he snapped the lid shut again. His grey eyes were watching her intently, and it was as though he were trying to read something deep down within her. It was a stare of abysmal quality.

'At least,' Pat said, trying to sound offhand, 'you might have let me look at it properly!'

'I will,' he said quietly. 'And I know just what you were going to say when you glimpsed it. It's wonderful! It ought to be! I've pinched and scraped good and hard to get it . . . I want to be sure my money hasn't been wasted.'

'Wasted! Well, of all the confounded — '

'Hear me out,' he interrupted. 'I want to know something. Am I the only man?'

Pat's heightened colour faded and the resentment went out of her eyes. She gave an incredulous laugh.

'The only man? Well, of course! Haven't we been walking out together for months?'

'Sure we have, but . . . ' Keith began walking again. Perforce Pat had to follow him. They passed from the main road into a quiet side street.

'I've an infernally jealous nature, you know,' he said suddenly. 'I'm wondering about Billy Cranston — and Cliff Evans. They've been very friendly with you. I can't help remembering that.'

'That doesn't mean anything.' Pat's attitude stiffened. There were limits as to how far she was prepared to make concessions. 'Look here, Keith, I'm not going to account to you for the various boys with whom I've been friendly — '

'All right!' he interrupted, his voice hard. 'I just can't help asking. You see, Pat, I love you so much I don't want to find later on that you would really rather have teamed up with Billy Cranston or Cliff Evans.'

'That's so absurd it isn't worth commenting upon,' Pat retorted. 'Any girl not knowing you as well as I do would have been ready to slap your face for the things you've said.'

Keith smiled. The gloomy mood that had been pervading him suddenly vanished. He took the ring from the case and

6

slipped it on her finger.

'That seals the bargain,' he said. 'Next thing we have to do is to see how our respective parents react. Not that it matters, anyway, since we're both of age, but I suppose one must try and get co-operation if at all possible.'

Pat admired the ring as they strolled along towards her home. 'There won't be any difficulty as far as my folks are concerned,' she said. 'And you've only your dad to worry about, haven't you?'

'Uh-huh — and it's more than enough.'

Pat's thoughts clouded. She had suddenly realized the kind of man she would have for a father-in-law. Ambrose Robinson lived in an aura of self-imposed austerity that would have made any Government official jealous. He was the plain-living, strait-laced type, obnoxiously proud of the fact that he never smoked, drank, or swore, and that he knew his Bible from cover to cover. But his seeming piety was flavoured with an intense bitterness towards the world in general and his son in particular.

'We shan't live with Dad, anyway,'

Keith said, and Pat knew he had been interpreting her thoughts. 'He's a psalm-smiting old humbug, and that's plain speaking . . . '

'Where *shall* we live?' Pat asked anxiously. 'We've only one spare guest-room and I can't see Mum giving it up to us. Besides, it never works out right to live with one's parents.'

'I'd thought of rooms in Gladstone Avenue,' Keith said, naming a fairly select quarter of the district. 'I'll be able to afford it. Not the kind of dream-home we'd like, perhaps, but it'll do for the time being. At least we'll be to ourselves.'

'Which means everything,' Pat agreed, and added in a matter-of-fact tone, 'When shall we get married?'

'I'm due for a rise in three months. How about then?'

Pat, whose thoughts were running on how quickly she could escape from her work in the restaurant, nodded promptly.

'That's fine! Can't be too soon for me.'

They had come to the end of the road where her home stood. It was No. 18 Cypress Avenue — one in a row of thirty identical houses, all with small front gardens, bay windows up and down, and a brick garage at the side.

'We'll tell my folks now,' Pat said. 'They should all be in.'

The large back living room was warm, the June sunlight partly blocked by half-drawn curtains. There was a homely untidiness about the place. Detective and crime magazines peeped out from surprising places; correspondence was wedged between the mantel clock and an empty decorated jar. On the chesterfield under the window Pat's father, a big, powerful man with a quasi-bald head and large stomach, was lounging as he read the evening paper. At the laid table Pat's brother Gregory was circumspectly dressed, toying with a salad.

'Is anything the matter, dear?' Mrs. Taylor asked. She was a large, blonde woman with the enviable gift of seeming always happy. Blue-eyed, double-chinned, her girth was emphasized by the huge spotless apron she was wearing. 'You look sort of — pent up!'

'We're engaged!' Pat said suddenly, and

thrust out her left hand as though it were a sword. 'Look!'

The silence of the room was broken now by a variety of sounds. Mr. Taylor's paper rustled as he lowered it to his paunch. A clink came from Gregory's plate as he put down his knife and fork. Mrs. Taylor breathed audibly.

'Engaged!' she exclaimed. 'You hear that, Harry?'

'I certainly do!' He came lumbering across the room to grip Keith by one hand and Pat by the other. 'Not that it's unexpected,' he said, smiling. 'The very best of luck to both of you. Mmm, nice ring, too! That put you back a bit, my boy.'

'For Pat it's worth it,' Keith responded.

Mrs. Taylor added her congratulations, and Keith began to look as though he found the business somewhat over-whelming. Being on the small side, the size of his future parents-in-law seemed rather gargantuan to him. Then the vision of expansive shirt and even more expansive bosom cleared from before him and gave place to Gregory Taylor's face — cold and lantern-jawed.

'Congratulations!' Gregory Taylor said laconically. He was a solicitor's clerk, and though only twenty-nine he looked fifty. Despite a shade temperature close on eighty-eight he was neatly dressed in a complete suit with spotless collar and tie. His eyes were a peculiar shade of light grey. His hair was so polished and flattened with vaseline it looked black, though actually was dark brown.

'You don't sound very enthusiastic, Greg,' Pat commented dryly. 'Or don't you realize how important this is?'

'You mean to you, of course?' her brother asked. 'I'm not marrying Keith.'

Pat hesitated — then Mr. Taylor startled everybody by slapping his palms together.

'A hot day and an engagement — this calls for a drink!' he declared. 'Mother, we've some port somewhere put aside for Christmas. Where is it?'

'In the cellar, dear. But what do we do for Christmas?'

'Buy some more, of course.' Mr. Taylor grinned widely. 'The cellar, eh? Right!

Keith, my boy, you're coming with me.'

Keith shrugged and followed Mr. Taylor's lumbering figure out of the room. Two strides took them across the hall to a door set in the side of the stairs. It was locked, a key projecting from it. Taylor turned the key, opened the door wide, and switched on the light at the top of a curving wooden staircase. He went down it briskly and Keith followed him. At the base of the stairs they came into the glow of the single electric bulb depending from a short flex.

Keith halted, looking about him, whilst Mr. Taylor went to the copper and from inside it took out a bottle of wine.

Absently Keith glanced around the cool, brick-walled, concrete-floored expanse. There was a rusty old wringer, a clothes-rope hanging on a nail, a chair without a back — and that was all. Mrs. Taylor preferred the depredations of a laundry to washing at home. The door that presumably led to a contiguous cellar had been screwed up. Nearly opposite the base of the staircase was an empty fireplace with rusty iron bars, and a wide old-fashioned type of chimney flue.

'Now, my lad . . . '

Keith gave a start. He had been looking at a staple in a beam that crossed the ceiling.

'Just a word,' Mr. Taylor said, his round pink face full of good humour. 'I'm mighty glad you're having Pat. I've got an idea about fixing a surprise present for you both later on.' He squeezed Keith's arm. 'You're just the right chap. Dammit, I've known your dad for years, haven't I?'

'I'm glad you approve,' Keith said, smiling awkwardly.

Returning to the living room they found that Mrs. Taylor had produced five wineglasses and was busy polishing them.

'It took you a long time, Harry,' she complained. 'What did you two have to talk about?'

'Never mind,' Mr. Taylor grinned, fishing a corkscrew out of the silver basket. In another moment he had the bottle open.

'Don't include me,' Gregory said. 'I don't like wine at the best of times, and certainly not in the middle of my tea.'

'Hang it all, Greg, the least you can do is drink to your sister's happiness,' Mr. Taylor complained, his huge bulk looming over the glasses as he filled them.

'Well . . . ' Gregory gave a sigh. 'All right — just this once.'

Raising the filled glasses, Mr. Taylor handed them over ceremoniously one by one. 'To both of you,' he said to Pat and Keith.

The wine was drunk and the glasses returned to the table. An impressive quiet dropped for a moment.

'I — I think this is mighty nice of all of you,' Keith said at last. 'I wasn't quite sure how you'd accept the idea, though of course you must have known that Pat and I felt that way about each other.'

'Yes, we knew,' Mrs. Taylor acknowledged, smiling. 'When is it to be?'

'We thought about three months,' Keith answered. 'When I get my next pay rise. I expect it'll be hard going at first trying to get settled down — but then, it's the same for all young couples these days. We'll get by.'

'Course you will!' Mr. Taylor declared

heartily. 'Getting married's a problem whichever way you look at it, but with support from parents on both sides you'll be all right.'

'Oh yes — of course.' Keith gave a peculiar smile to himself and made a half move towards the door. 'I'd better get along and tell Dad what's happened. He won't approve, of course — '

'I'll go home with you,' Pat intervened. 'If he won't listen to you he will to me. I'll see to that!'

'But what about your tea, dear?' her mother exclaimed.

'I'll have tea when I get back.' Pat smiled. She caught Keith's arm impulsively. 'Come along, Keith — let's go and tell your dad.'

'As you like, but I'm afraid he'll take it the hard way.'

They left the room with their arms about each other. Mr. Taylor gazed absently before him and pulled out his pipe.

'Funny thing,' he mused, 'you can sort of picture marriage and home-leaving happening to other people's children but not to your own.'

'It's a pity Pat doesn't use her head a bit more,' Gregory said He folded his table napkin neatly and laid it on one side. His father gazed down on him thoughtfully.

'Use her head, Greg? How d'you mean?'

'Simply that there are hundreds of men who'd make her a much better husband than Keith Robinson.' Gregory frowned. 'It isn't that I've anything against him, only from things he's said now and again when he's been here I think he's got an insanely jealous disposition. And people like that are hell to live with.'

'How do you know?' His father gave a wide grin. 'You never lived with such a person.'

'I'm thinking of Pat's happiness, and with Keith I can't see her having any after the novelty's worn off. Deep down, I think she's only in love with a handsome face.' Gregory got to his feet. 'Now, if you don't mind, I'll go up to my room and browse through those confounded law books. I've a problem on my mind at the office.'

He closed the door behind him. Mr. Taylor lighted his pipe slowly and puffed at it. Presently he looked at his wife as she began to move the tray containing the empty glasses towards the adjoining kitchen.

'Think Pat's doing the wrong thing, Alice?' he asked.

'Not for a moment! She's no child, Harry. Oh, take no notice of Greg! He spends most of his life looking for the faults in people. Why, you're not beginning to have doubts, are you?'

'Not I — only Greg has the uncomfortable habit of upsetting one's applecart so completely. Maybe his disliking Keith has a lot to do with it.'

Mrs. Taylor gave a shrug of her fleshy shoulders and then went on into the kitchen. Her husband followed her.

'Y'know, I think we should have a really good celebration!' he declared. 'Pat can invite her friends and Keith can invite his — and bring his father over. A really good get-together, eh? A proper engagement party!'

Clearly the idea appealed to Mrs.

Taylor's sociable soul. 'We'll tell Pat about it the moment she comes in,' she nodded. 'She'll be delighted . . . Then she must make a list of who she wants to invite.'

2

Pat and Keith talked all the way to his home, a journey of perhaps a mile to the centre of the town. They paused at last outside a shop in Ridley Terrace, lying directly off the main street. On the front window it said — *Ambrose Robinson. Ironmonger and Locksmith. Keys Made to Order.*

'Now for it,' Keith murmured, grasping Pat's arm.

He unlocked the house door at the side — the shop itself being closed at six — and led the way through a narrow hall into the back room, which comprised the living quarters. Ambrose Robinson was present — a lean-faced man with thin grey hair, seated at the table, eating a meal. Propped before him against the teapot was a volume on religious revival on the Dark Continent.

'Hello, Dad,' Keith greeted. 'I've a visitor to see you.'

Ambrose Robinson looked at Pat and got to his feet. He was extremely tall and his hand seemed, as he extended it, to be as fleshless as a skeleton's.

'Oh, it's you, Pat.' He had a sombre, judicial way of speaking. 'Quite a while since I've seen you. Be the last time I called on your father, I think.'

'It was,' Pat agreed, with a nervous little smile. 'But of course Keith and I have seen a lot of each other in the interval . . . '

'Really?' Ambrose Robinson said, with intense quietness. 'I didn't know that.'

For some reason Pat always found that the gaunt, lanky ironmonger made her feel scared. Perhaps it was his irresistible resemblance to a vulture, typified in his hooked nose and jutting chin, the prominent eyes boring down from the great height.

Keith broke the impasse. 'Pat and I are engaged, Dad. That's why I brought her along to see you. I felt it was only right that I should.'

Ambrose Robinson regained his chair and sank down into it. 'Engaged?' he repeated.

20

'That's what I said. See!' Keith caught Pat's hand and Ambrose Robinson gazed at the ring aghast.

' "The Lord giveth and the Lord taketh away",' he half-mumbled to himself. 'You're all I've *got*, Keith! Why did you have to do this? With your poor mother gone I was hoping that you and I — '

'It can't be a surprise to you!' Keith broke in, his tone suddenly rough. 'I've my own life to live and if I've decided to get married, that's the end of it. At least you might congratulate us!'

Pat gave Keith a wondering glance. 'Did you need to fly off the handle like that? You haven't even given your dad a chance to speak yet.'

'Be all same if I had!' Keith snapped.

Ambrose Robinson got to his feet again and took hold of Pat's hand. He looked at Keith. 'You've chosen Pat . . . All right, that's the end of it.'

Pat found herself kissed lightly on the cheek and tried not to wince. For some reason Ambrose Robinson looked at her in sudden sharpness. Then he said:

'I wish it hadn't been Keith, that's all.'

Pat smiled uncomfortably. 'But it *is*, Mr. Robinson! And I'm glad of it. After all, we've no intention of leaving town or anything like that. We're hoping to get some rooms in Gladstone Avenue, so we'll be quite near. Remember the old saying — you're not losing a son, you're gaining a daughter.'

'As far as I am concerned, Pat, I am losing a son. No more, no less . . . Don't misunderstand,' Ambrose Robinson added. 'I like you Pat; I know you and your family well; only . . . Well, perhaps I've sort of become selfish, regarded Keith as my own precious possession. I've always feared this would happen one day, yet now it is here I — I just don't know what to say or think.' He sighed. 'So be it . . . 'He that is greedy of gain troubleth his own house.' That's from Proverbs,' he explained, and sat down again.

Pat gave Keith a glance. 'Keith, don't you think — '

What Pat thought was never expressed, for at that moment Keith Robinson fainted.

There was no warning beyond his

rubbing his forehead once or twice, then suddenly his knees gave way and he fell flat on his face. Pat stared down at him in horror.

'It's this confoundedly hot room!' Ambrose Robinson declared, jumping up. 'Keith never could stand a hot room.' He stooped, lifted Keith's slight body across to the sofa and eased him onto it. Then he opened his collar.

Without being told, Pat hurried out into the back kitchen and returned with water in a basin. Ambrose Robinson whipped up his napkin from the table and dipped it in the water, began to smooth it across Keith's forehead. He stirred but did not revive.

'Shall I get a doctor?' Pat asked urgently

Ambrose Robinson held Keith's wrist gently, taking his pulse. 'No,' he said finally; 'he'll be all right in a while. I can handle him.' He turned towards Pat again. 'I think you'd better go, Pat,' he said deliberately.

'But I don't want to go! I want to be sure he's all right. I can't think what made him pass out like that . . . '

'I can,' Ambrose Robinson said. 'Drink! His breath is defiled with it — and so is yours!' He got to his feet and towered over the girl. 'I noticed it when I kissed you. Where have you led my boy? What do you plan to do to do to him?'

Pat gestured helplessly. 'But — but it's nothing. We drank some wine. My dad insisted that we should — to celebrate.'

'You behold the result!' Ambrose Robinson snapped, pointing a bony finger at Keith. 'To the best of my knowledge Keith has never taken intoxicant in his life. Wine — a hot room — and the fact that he is not an overstrong young man . . . So he collapsed. 'My heart is smitten and withered like grass.' Psalms.'

'What's that got to do with it?' Pat demanded angrily.

'Young woman,' Ambrose Robinson said coldly, 'You have chosen to become engaged to my son. Inevitably his feet will be directed out of the narrow path I had chosen for him. This is the beginning: that he falls under the curse of drink.'

'A glass of wine isn't the curse of drink!

It's just Keith's hard luck that he couldn't stand it . . . And I'm staying until he comes round.'

'No! You are leaving, Pat — and 'confounded be they that serve graven images'!'

Pat hesitated, looked again at the deeply sleeping, sprawled figure, then without another word she turned and went.

With a harassed face she returned home through the quiet, hot streets. The moments with Ambrose Robinson had been intensely disturbing. Her expression gave her away the moment she entered the living room at home.

'Say, wait a minute,' her father said, tossing aside his newspaper and getting up from the chesterfield. 'What's happened to you, Pat? You look as though you're nearing crying.'

'I am!' she declared fiercely, and burst out weeping as she threw herself down at the table. Irritably she pushed away the plate that had been laid for her tea.

'Have you quarrelled?' her father asked.

'No,' Pat mumbled, her face buried.

Her mother put an arm about her shoulders. 'What *is* it, dear? What's wrong?'

'It's all because you gave Keith that wine!' Pat complained, looking up, and between gasps she got out the whole story. Instead of her father looking contrite, he began to laugh.

'When did it happen?' he asked, chuckling. 'In the street?'

'No. We'd been in the house about ten minutes and it isn't funny either, Dad!' Pat objected, her own tears beginning to cease.

'Isn't it, my girl?' Her father laughed. 'Gosh, I can just imagine the face of that religious old fathead when his son passed out through quaffing the Devil's brew. Do old Ambrose good!' he snorted. 'He's always trying to look like the archangel Gabriel while he spouts his yards of memorized scripture. 'Bout time he got acquainted with the facts of life.'

'But, Dad, what do we do about Keith?'

Mr. Taylor's laughter subsided into a grin. 'He'll be all right,' he said. 'He'll sleep it off. Evidently he's got the kind of mollycoddled constitution that folds up under a drink. Some people have. Won't do the lad any harm. As for Ambrose, forget him. Next time I see him I'll tell him exactly what I think.' Pat found her shoulders shaken with an understanding roughness. 'Smile, girl, smile! You're engaged! There's only one solution to a drink knocking you out cold — have a bigger drink next time.'

'After all, Harry, that isn't very practical,' Mrs. Taylor said seriously.

'If you'd been to as many engineering conventions as I have you'd know it's the only answer . . . Listen, Pat, get on with your tea and hear about a scheme your mum and I have thought up.'

By degrees the infection of Mr. Taylor's good spirits began to tell and Pat even found herself laughing too at the thought of Keith laid out through celebrating his engagement. She drew her plate, knife and fork back to her and tackled her salad. Her father and mother returned to either side of the table.

'Keith might as well get in practice,'

Mr. Taylor said dryly, 'because there's a big celebration coming up — say on Wednesday next week. You'll be at home from noon and it will give you plenty of chance to doll up. Greg will also be home early on Wednesday, and so shall I.'

'You mean we're going to throw a party?' Pat asked, in sudden excitement. 'Who'll be coming?'

'Everybody that matters. Keith, his father, and you'll want to dig up some of your own friends. What about those two boys who've been following you around with cow-eyes for the last few months?'

'Them?' Pat shook her head. 'No, I don't think so. Keith's a bit jealous of them already: it would be throwing fat in the fire to ask them to a party with him present, too.'

'Oh . . . ' Her father shrugged. 'Up to you.'

Pat said: 'I'll invite Madge Banning for one. She's my best friend and relief cashier at the restaurant. And there's Betty Andrews. She used to be at Roseway with me. I want her and Madge Banning to be my bridesmaids — they'd love a celebration.'

'They shall have it. I'll get some wine and we — '

'No wine, Dad,' Pat said seriously. 'Not after what happened to Keith tonight. Please — *no wine*. Let's have non-intoxicants — ginger beer, lemonade, or something like that. Suppose Keith — or even Madge or Betty — passed out? Mr. Robinson would recite the entire Book of Psalms to us!'

Mr. Taylor grinned. 'All right then — lemonade . . . Now, anybody else you want to come?'

Pat smiled faintly. 'Yes, just one person. Miss Black, my old headmistress. She has friends in Redford she can stay with.'

Mr. Taylor looked dubious. 'Miss Black? I can't see how your former headmistress can bring joy to the proceedings. More likely to prove a wet blanket.'

'Not Miss Black,' Pat answered. 'There wasn't a girl in the college who didn't like her — at the time I was there — and I don't think she's changed much. I'd love her to come. She'll be highly interested in my getting married.'

'Langhorn, in Sussex, is a good fifty miles from here,' Mr. Taylor pointed out. 'Do you think she'd — '

'Don't start raking up obstacles, Dad! She's got a little Austin Seven — '

'How do you know that?'

'Oh, I write to her now and again,' Pat said airily. 'You know, problems I can't solve myself and which I — ' Pat hesitated '— and which I don't want to bother you or Mum with.'

'I like that!' her mother exclaimed. 'The child's got a second mother pushed away and we never guessed . . . ' Then she laughed. 'All right, Pat, you ask her. As I remember her she will be an asset to any party — even if only to put old Ambrose where he belongs. By the way, doesn't she dabble in crime study or something?'

'It's her hobby,' Pat said. 'But surely that hasn't anything to do with it?'

'Nothing in my shady past which will interest the lady, anyway,' Mr. Taylor commented, grinning. 'And a headmistress who is a criminologist sounds crazy to me. Dabbler, I suppose.'

'A dabbler who's solved many cases which the police could not,' Pat stated proudly. 'That's why I keep on writing to her — apart from the personal problems I raise.'

Her father stared at her. 'What on earth are you talking about?'

'Crime, of course. It's everywhere these days — in books, magazines, films and real life. I'm interested in it — and there is no doubt that Greg is. I often wonder if anybody will ever commit the perfect crime . . . '

'What next?' Mrs. Taylor sighed. 'Even supposing somebody did, it would be so perfect nobody would know anything about it . . . Now finish your tea dear, then maybe you'd better write to Miss Black and Betty and see what they have to say.'

* * *

Keith Robinson opened an eye. It closed again before the naked brilliance of electric light. He reopened it more slowly and the other eye with it. He was looking at a silhouette of his father against the light. He was reading something lying on his bony knees . . . A Bible. Keith's eyes strayed beyond his father to the clock on the mantelshelf. It said eleven. There was dull pain at the back of his head and a vile taste in his mouth.

'What happened?' he whispered, sitting up.

His father laid aside the Bible on the table. 'This is what you get for becoming engaged to a girl who loves this world's pleasures,' he said bitterly. 'You drank some wine, and it proved too much for you.'

Keith pressed finger and thumb to his eyes. 'The wine . . . Of course! And have I got a hangover! I — I passed out, then?'

'You passed out.' Long pause. 'Keith, we've got to talk this thing over. You're planning to marry a girl who drinks and I know her father does. I cannot let you throw yourself away on such a girl — '

'There's nothing the matter with Pat!' Keith said angrily. 'One drink doesn't matter. It's I who am the fool not to have been able to stand it. And you can't tell me what to do, Dad. We've never hit it off, and parting is about the best thing that could happen for both of us.'

'Have you no gratitude, boy?' Ambrose Robinson whispered. 'Have I not brought you up? Have I not guarded you? Have I not — '

Keith sat upright. 'I've spent all my life, when at home, listening to your everlasting psalm-singing about the evils of the world and the baseness of everybody except yourself. Even if I had not decided to marry Pat, I would have walked out on you. You don't see as much of life as I do. You're cooped up in this little ironmongery shop, passing judgment on your customers and spending the rest of your time reading Scripture. That isn't religion; it's self-centred bigotry. Down at the station I see folk as they are, and as I mean my own children to be, if I have any. All this may sound callous but — I'm *sick* of you!'

' "When the wicked spring as the grass it is they who shall be destroyed for ever — " '

Keith stood up. 'I won't listen to such stuff any longer. Where's Pat gone?'

'I told her to leave.'

'You *told* her to! By what right?'

'By the right of a father. Don't you realize what you are doing, boy? You are marrying a woman whose first thought upon becoming engaged was to make you insensible with drink!'

'It was Mr. Taylor's idea,' Keith said sourly. 'And even if I did pass out it was only a single glass. Don't start magnifying things. I'll drink if I want to — and I'll smoke — and if the necessity arises I'll swear! You're living in a world that just doesn't exist beyond these walls, Dad.'

'That you should say such things to me,' Ambrose Robinson whispered. 'Would that your poor dear mother were alive.'

'Yes . . . ' Keith stared absently. 'Would that she were. She'd understand just how I feel. You're driving me out just the same as you drove her to her death.'

Ambrose Robinson looked up sharply. 'You have the brazen insolence to suggest that I caused her to pass away?'

'That's right.' Keith's handsome face was cynical. 'I can remember your psalm-smiting, the way you treated her, the money you kept back from her, the way you crushed out every little thing she treasured.'

'I have always lived to a rule, boy, and I always shall. In the name of decency keep your mother's name out of this — '

'It's true!' Keith snapped. 'Your parsimony was directly responsible for her death. Oh, I know you spun a fancy tale about her dying peacefully in the Sunbeam Home of Rest after a long illness. I know that was the story you told everybody — including Pat's father and Aunt Lydia. It made you look the injured party. I don't forget these things even if you do. Mother's memory is sacred to me, and the only thing I regret is that you and I didn't part sooner.'

Silence. The clock chimed quarter past eleven. Keith's father got to his feet and brooded.

'You have things mixed up, Keith,' he said at length. 'I didn't drive your mother to her death. It was — '

'Let it drop!' Keith interrupted harshly. 'I've had my own views about it ever since I was old enough to think for myself.'

' 'Hatred stirreth up strifes, but love covereth all sins',' Ambrose Robinson muttered; and added, 'Proverbs.'

Keith controlled an utterance and looked at the empty table. He went into the back kitchen and spent a few minutes getting together a supper for himself. He was seated eating it before his father spoke again.

'I take it, then, that you'll be leaving?'

'Once I'm married nothing will stop me. I can't go until then, unfortunately, because there's nowhere to go ... ' Keith's grey eyes met his father's across the table. 'Don't think I'm staying on here because of any consideration for you.'

'We have never understood each other,' Ambrose Robinson declared bitterly.

'You don't understand anybody, nor do you try. Religion, the way you handle it, is plain poison.'

Ambrose Robinson meditated. 'You're satisfied that you are doing the right thing in marrying Pat Taylor?'

'Perfectly.' Keith smiled cynically. 'Even if she does take a glass of wine; so don't start that again!'

'I wasn't thinking of that: she will suffer for whatever sins she commits, just as you will. I was wondering if she knows you half as well as you think she does. You are a strange boy, Keith. You're utterly jealous. You have strange fancies and moods. I cannot visualize you as the ideal partner for any girl. For that reason, amongst others, I have tried to dissuade you from all thought of marriage.'

'I'm not sitting here any longer listening to your drivel!' Keith shouted, jumping up. 'What's it got to do with you how I behave or what I do? Look at home, Dad: there's plenty wants altering! *I'm going to bed!*'

He strode out and slammed the door. His father sat thinking, his lips tight.

'"A wise son heareth his father's instruction",' he muttered, '"but a scorner heareth not rebuke . . . " Proverbs.'

3

The following day Pat met Keith as usual at the restaurant on his return from work, and once he had reassured her that his recovery from the glass of wine was complete she plunged into details of the intended celebration party on the following Wednesday. That he would be there was a certainty — but he was not so sure about his father.

'But you must bring him!' Pat insisted. 'It's Dad's idea. After all, I suppose my dad and yours want to get together and discuss things. You know how it is.'

'Yes, I know,' Keith said moodily. 'Can't keep their noses out of their children's affairs.'

'Oh, Keith, I'm sure it isn't that bad — '

'Yes it is,' he insisted curtly. Then he shrugged. 'All right, I'll ask Dad and he can please himself. I'm also going to see if I can't get my raise in under three months, then we can be married sooner. Every day I spend with the old man I get more nervy . . . ' He switched the subject suddenly. 'I hope you've told Billy Cranston and Cliff Evans that they needn't call on you any more? That we're engaged?'

'No, I haven't,' Pat answered coolly. 'They haven't called, and I'm certainly not going to run about after them. And do you *have* to be so confoundedly jealous?'

'Can't help it,' he replied. 'And tell 'em as soon as you can, Pat. If either of them try and remain friendly with you from now I won't be responsible for my actions.'

'You won't what?' Pat exclaimed in amazement.

'I . . . Perhaps I put it badly,' he amended. 'What I mean is, I just can't stomach the idea of any other men being interested in you when you belong to me. Can't help my nature, can I?'

Pat was silent. It had suddenly crossed her mind that perhaps she was making a mistake after all. This intense jealousy in

Keith's make-up was likely to grow deeper as the years passed and it might lead to unpredictable consequences.

'I sound worse than I am,' Keith added, grinning. 'Moody — that's me! After all, it's a sure sign that I love you when I'm jealous, isn't it?'

Pat smiled faintly. The thought that none of us is perfect took precedence in her mind again. For all his jealousy, queer little ways, and startling changes of mood, Keith fascinated her. She was still not at an age to adopt searching self-analysis and ask herself whether it was Keith himself, or his handsome looks, which really appealed to her. But the fact remained that she was determined to marry him . . .

She saw him each evening thereafter, and at the weekend. Evidently he had smoothed things out at home to a certain extent, for on the Wednesday following, precisely at six o'clock, he arrived with his father at the Taylor home. With a kind of forced cheerfulness he followed his gaunt death's-head of a parent into the big front room, and then paused. There were so many people present he seemed momentarily to be at a loss.

Pat, fetchingly attired in a frilly party dress and with a gentle perfume clinging about her, came forward to grasp his hand. At the same moment Mr. Taylor, who had been considering the lemonade and glasses on the table, lumbered over and gripped Ambrose Robinson's bony claw.

'More we are together, eh?' Mr. Taylor exclaimed genially. 'Glad you decided to come, Ambrose. After all, your son and my daughter. It's a tremendous occasion!'

'I came because I was invited,' Ambrose Robinson told him sombrely; 'Certainly not because I think I've anything to celebrate. Indeed, I have nothing to celebrate in losing my son.'

'Er — let me introduce you, Mr. Robinson,' Pat intervened. 'This is Miss Banning, a great friend of mine and also a fellow worker; and this is Miss Andrews, an old school friend. Both of them are to be my bridesmaids.'

Ambrose Robinson smiled down gauntly on the two young women and then nodded

41

to Gregory Taylor. Gregory was lounging in a corner armchair, smoking a cigarette impassively without a trace of expression on his wooden-looking face.

'Don't take it so hard, Ambrose!' Mrs. Taylor murmured, smiling, as he drifted to her side. 'It makes it so tough on the young people when their parents don't agree with the marrying. What in the world have you to object to, anyway?'

'Oh, it's nothing personal,' Ambrose Robinson responded. 'It's just that I find it hard to lose Keith after all the plans I'd been making to direct his future. I think he's treading on the wrong path.'

'Not with our daughter!' Mr. Taylor declared. 'You've been reading your Bible upside down, Ambrose.'

'There is nothing wrong with reading a Bible,' Ambrose Robinson retorted. 'You might try it yourself some time!'

Mr. Taylor hesitated and then glanced about him. 'Well,' he said, 'we all seem to be here except Miss Black . . . Oh, Pat, you didn't invite Billy Cranston or Cliff Evans, those two boyfriends of yours, did you?'

Pat coloured swiftly and Keith's mouth hardened visibly.

'No,' she responded. 'Why should I? They don't really mean anything . . . '

Mr. Taylor winked. 'So you say!' He turned to his wife. 'Well, Mother, what do we do about the drinks? The longer we delay having them the longer we'll be getting to the fun and games. And believe me,' he added, turning to the assembly, 'I've worked out plenty of fun for this evening. You'll never forget it.'

'But we can't have the drinks yet, Dad,' Pat objected. 'We really must wait for Miss Black. She ought to be here at any moment.'

'According to her letter,' Gregory said, looking at his wristwatch, 'she should have been here forty-five minutes ago.'

Pat shrugged. 'Well, you know how it is with a car. Maybe she broke down. Normally she's a terror for punctuality.'

'Miss Black?' repeated Ambrose Robinson vaguely. 'Do I know her?'

Pat shook her head. 'You've never met her. Neither has Keith. She's the headmistress of Roseway College, where I

43

used to be. I know you'll like her . . . '

Silence. The ticking clock could be heard distinctly. For a moment or two Mr. Taylor looked at a loss.

'What do we do then?' he complained. 'The longer we delay the less time we'll have . . . '

Since, however, it was Pat's party she had the authority, and she managed to delay the drinks for another half-hour; then as there was still no sign of Miss Maria Black she had to give way and the party started in earnest.

Thanks to the vigorous good nature of Mr. Taylor, the first icy reserve was soon broken. The Misses Banning and Andrews got to giggling by turns, and Keith seemed to have thrown his moodiness overboard and replaced it with a widely smiling countenance. Even the solemn, funereal gloom of his father broke down somewhat, but to the convulsive delight of Madge Banning it did not prevent him uttering Biblical phrases at intervals. Only Gregory Taylor remained unmoved, though he drank with the rest and repeated the toast to the engaged pair as though he were taking the oath in court.

The room grew hot and smoky and voices blurred across the clink of glasses. The mountains of sandwiches and home-made cakes and buns went the round of the gathering as if on a conveyor belt.

Pat, conversing on some feminine topic with the Misses Banning and Andrews, realized suddenly that she could not see Keith anywhere. His father was still present, discoursing into the unheeding ear of Mrs. Taylor about the flight of the Israelites through the Red Sea. There was Mr. Taylor; trying to make himself heard about some games he had devised in the next room . . .

'Where's Keith?' Pat asked suddenly, getting up and looking about her.

'I dunno.' Her father looked surprised. 'Slipped out for a moment, I suppose. Look, all of you, let's go in the next room and we can — '

'But I want to ask him something!' Pat insisted. 'What's he up to, I wonder?'

'Last I saw of him he was talking to you, Dad,' Gregory said, from the armchair.

'Yes, but — ' Mr. Taylor frowned ' — that was ten minutes ago . . . '

Pat left the room worriedly and the conversation went on, though not quite at the same tempo. From the expressions on their faces everybody seemed to be thinking the same thing. At last Pat came back into the hot, smoky atmosphere.

'He's nowhere in the house!' she announced in dismay. 'I've searched every room, upstairs and down — he must have walked out . . . '

'He couldn't have!' Ambrose Robinson declared. 'I'll find him! I know his little tricks . . . '

He left the room and was gone for perhaps fifteen minutes. He returned with an expression of puzzlement and alarm that was only equalled by Pat's own.

'Can't find him anywhere,' Ambrose Robinson said, rubbing his eyebrow. 'I just don't understand it. Why should he walk out?'

'But he can't have done that!' Mr. Taylor exclaimed. 'He must be up to some prank or other. Come on; we'll all have a look.'

The party all crowded out of the drawing room and dispersed in various directions to undertake the search, which, for Pat and Ambrose Robinson, had already proved fruitless. Even the garage and outhouses were not ignored, but there was still no sign of Keith anywhere.

'If he went out we'd have seen him go down the front path,' Betty Andrews said brightly.

'I just can't understand it,' Ambrose Robinson said, as they congregated in the hall.

'Neither can I,' Mr. Taylor added, frowning. Then an inspiration seemed to strike him. 'Say, what about the cellar? Anybody look there?'

From the shaking of heads it appeared nobody had.

'Then let's have a look there.' Her father moved to the cellar door in the staircase.

Turning the knob, he fell back in surprise as the door remained secure. 'The mystery's solved!' he exclaimed. 'Keith's up to something in the cellar. He must be. He — '

'Say, look!' Gregory pointed. 'There's a gleam of light under the cellar door there — A faint line . . . What the blazes can he be playing at?'

'Key's gone: must be inside the door.' Mr. Taylor spoke as though sudden alarm had got him. 'Usually there's a key on the outside of this door . . . Gone! See?' He pointed. Then he thumped the panels fiercely.

'Hey, Keith! What goes on?'

No response. Pat, seized with a sudden premonition, gave a startled cry.

'Something may have happened to him! Smash the door, Dad.'

Without hesitation he slammed his massive body into it. It creaked but it did not give. Gregory lent his shoulders. Under the combined onslaught the door flew open and nearly flung Mr. Taylor down the steps beyond. He brought up sharp, clinging to both sides of the doorframe. He remained motionless. There was a deadly silence for a moment or two.

As Gregory had noticed, the light was on, but from this point at the top of the wooden stairway the bulb itself was not visible — only the brilliance casting from beyond the point where the wall jutted out at the base of the curving stairway. Nobody was noticing this, however. Their eyes were fixed on a shadow on the left-hand wall of the stairway.

It was the shadow of a man, hanging. A black line extended tautly upwards from his neck to the ceiling.

★　★　★

Meanwhile, Miss Maria Black, M.A., Principal of Roseway College for Young Ladies, was experiencing a shock of another kind. Briefly, her Austin Seven had mysteriously become immobile.

She had left the college in Sussex in ample time, and had proceeded to within twenty miles of her destination in Redford. Now she sat at the steering wheel, gazing in front of her and wondering what to do next.

With a sigh she squeezed out of the car and stood erect, a massive-bosomed woman in the late fifties attired in a fashionable two-piece, with a stylish hat perched on her severely coiffured hair. Her hair was greying black and ended in a bun at the nape of her short, strong neck.

She drew off her gloves tossed them into the car, and then with masculine strength and purpose heaved up the side of the bonnet. With eyes the colour of a blue glacier she considered the Austin's innards. There seemed to be a lot of oil-filmed metal and that was about all.

Understanding a car's engine was not one of Maria Black's accomplishments. She understood fractious young ladies and criminal minds a great deal better.

With an effort Maria cast aside her reluctance to fiddle with the oily mess and began an investigation, tapping the carburetor, plugs, distributor, and everything else she could find. She was thus engaged when she became aware of a squeak of brakes and the scrape of tyres on gravel surface. A young man climbed out of an ancient two-seater and came over to her.

'Trouble, ma'm?' he asked.

Maria straightened up, her dignity marred, had she but known it, by a smear of oil that looked startlingly like a moustache. Except for this unique addition her features were keen. Her mouth and jaw were firm without being cruel: her nose was long and straight, and definitely inquisitive. When she spoke she could not help sounding superior. It was born in her.

'I can assure you, young man, that I am not doing this for my own entertainment.'

The young man grinned. 'As it 'appens I know a bit about cars. I'll take a look if you like.'

Maria nodded thankfully and stood aside, studying her messy hands distastefully. The young man did something to the engine that she could not see.

' 'Ere's your trouble,' he exclaimed at length. 'A wire to your distributor is corroded. Ought to 'ave the wirin' checked now and again. Soon 'ave you going now.'

Maria pulled a duster from the dashboard cubby, wiped her hands, threw the duster away, and then waited. In five minutes the young man had the car started. Maria beamed on him.

'Splendid, young man! Every man to his trade. And how much am I in your debt?'

'Only too 'appy,' he replied, shrugging. 'No job for a lady of your class, anyway.'

He held the door open for her and she settled at the steering wheel again, as upright as a general on his charger. The engine was now ticking over sweetly.

'Thank you again, young man,' she said, still beaming — and then she started the car off down the road at ever-gathering speed. The clock showed her she had lost a valuable hour and ten minutes. It annoyed her. If there was one thing on which she prided herself it was punctuality.

4

Suddenly, as she stared at the wall and the shadow of the hanging figure, Pat Taylor gave a hoarse shout that rose into a scream.

'It's Keith! He's gone down there and — '

'Back!' her father snapped, stopping her from hurling herself forward down the wooden staircase. 'Get back, all of you! There's something horrible here . . . '

He forced them away by main strength and closed the door.

There was perspiration gleaming on his plump face. The eyes of the Misses Banning and Andrews were round in horror. They had only glimpsed but they had seen enough.

Pat who had apparently guessed the truth, turned suddenly grey and fainted. In a moment her mother was fussing over her, half-dragging her away from the little group in the hall.

'Get the doctor,' Mr. Taylor snapped suddenly to Gregory. 'Hurry up, lad.'

'Okay — and the police?'

'I — I don't know — '

'I do!' Gregory said, suddenly calm with his legal mind ticking over smoothly. 'It looks to me like plain suicide, but it could be murder . . . I'll call the police, too,' he decided, turned actively.

'Keith!' Ambrose Robinson whispered, staring dazedly after Gregory as he dashed past him. 'He's — he's hanged himself! *Hanged* himself! If it *is* him . . . But it must be! I've got to see him — '

'Better let me do it,' Taylor said grimly. 'No job for you, he being your son.'

Ambrose Robinson hesitated and Mr. Taylor suddenly became the captain of the ship.

'Get back in the front room, all of you,' he ordered. 'I'll attend to Keith. After all, this is my house. Mother, get these two girls to help you with Pat . . . '

He opened the cellar door again and swung it to behind him as he hurried down the steps. Those in the hall had hardly got into the drawing room with the unconscious Pat before Gregory came speeding back. He dived straight for the cellar door pushed it to after him, since the lock was half off, and then hurried down the curving staircase. On the wall his father's shadow had been added to that of the hanging figure. His father's arm was working vigorously.

Gregory hesitated for a moment, shocked out of his usual cold reserve. His father was standing on the solitary backless chair that was the only piece of furniture in the basement. Keith Robinson was hanging from the massively thick central beam crossing the ceiling. In the beam was a rusty staple and to this had been securely knotted the clothes-rope from which the body was swinging.

'Have you a knife or something?' Taylor panted. 'These knots are too tough for me.'

Gregory handed his penknife up, the blade open. His father sawed through the rope frantically and the strands finally gave. Between them they lowered the dead weight to the floor and tugged free the slipknot that had been drawn with savage tightness about the neck. The flesh of the neck was severely abrased. Keith's eyes were staring, his tongue was lolling out. His face had turned a deep purple.

'This is awful, Dad!' Gregory whispered. 'Is he — ?'

'Yes — he's dead.' Taylor lowered the limp hand and tightened his lips. 'Have to wait for Dr. Standish.'

'He'll be here any minute,' Gregory said. 'And the police too. In any case, Dr. Standish is the police surgeon, so it's all the same.'

'Why — the police?'

'It's suicide, isn't it? Keith mightn't have been dead, and in that case he could have been charged with *felo de se*. It might even have been murder . . . but don't ask me how.'

Mr. Taylor got to his feet. Gregory did likewise. Mr. Taylor studied the cellar thoughtfully and looked up at the rope he had cut. Then he glanced at the wall.

'He used the clothes-rope which was hanging there,' he said slowly. 'Then he must have stood on the chair, kicked it away from him, and — that was that. I found the chair overturned.'

Gregory looked as if he were trying to get his legal mind into focus. His father glanced up towards the doorway as there came sounds on the front path, echoing heavily at this depth. He heard the front doorbell ring. Hurried feet. Mr. Taylor moved forward to look up the curve of the staircase and saw a plump little man with a black bag hurrying down it.

'Afraid you're too late, Doctor,' Mr. Taylor said quietly; and to Gregory he added, 'Get upstairs, Greg, and tell them all what's happened. And do it gently. They'll have to know the facts.'

Gregory returned swiftly up the staircase, closing the door at the top. Without a word Dr. Standish went down on one knee and examined the body carefully. Taylor stood waiting and watching.

'Yes,' the medico said finally, rising and dusting his knees. 'Strangulation all right. The neck shows it, too. Apparently no bruises or other marks . . . You've advised the police, Mr. Taylor?'

'They should be here at any moment.'

'They won't particularly approve of your having cut the body down,' the doctor said.

'Won't they?' Mr. Taylor laughed shortly. 'Good God, what was I supposed to do? Let him hang? There might have been life in him. We could perhaps have saved him.'

'You should have tested his pulse first.'

'I was too confoundedly staggered to think of a thing like that . . . This is the most horrible thing I've ever witnessed. He must have come down here, locked himself in, and then hanged himself. Right in the middle of celebrating his engagement to Pat, too!'

'Oh?' Dr. Standish shook his head. 'Mmm, that *is* devilish, and no mistake — '

He stopped talking and turned his face expectantly. There was a pounding from the front path, the ringing of the doorbell, and then voices. In a moment or two the uniformed figures of Superintendent Haslow and Sergeant Catterall of the local police force came in view . . .

Maria Black was astonished upon

arriving in Cypress Avenue to behold an official police car outside the gate of her destination. She was so absorbed by the sight she nearly forgot to jam on the brakes, and stopped the Austin Seven only a couple of inches from the police car's rear bumper. Then she sat gazing at No. 18. There was no policeman visible, except the one in the peaked uniform-cap at the wheel of the car. She did notice, however, that faces were peeping through lace curtains in the other houses and that children were watching from a safe distance.

Maria could feel her pulses tingling. Of course, the whole thing might be a coincidence. It did not say that anything was wrong in No. 18 just because a police car had parked outside it.

She considered herself in the driving mirror, removed the oil-moustache from her upper lip, then climbed out of the car. With dignified steps she walked along the pavement to the police car and looked in on the waiting driver.

'Is there anything — er — wrong at No. 18, officer?' she questioned.

'The Super and Sergeant are in there, madam. A suicide, I understand.'

'A suicide?' Maria's eyebrows rose; then she recovered her dignity, and turned to the gateway. Her ringing at the front door brought the sergeant to open it.

'Yes?' he asked respectfully, and met a steady look from ice-blue eyes.

'I am Miss Black,' Maria stated calmly. 'Miss Taylor is expecting me.'

The sergeant seemed to be aware of this fact. He nodded and stood to one side, motioning Maria into the hall. From here she was conducted into the front room. Three pale-faced young women were seated on a chesterfield; a youngish man with polished dark hair was in an armchair; a man like a vulture was standing with his hands clasped behind his back and his head bowed. A Superintendent of Police was considering something as he stood opposite a stout blonde woman and a good-natured-looking man.

'Miss Black!' the centre girl on the chesterfield exclaimed, and came hurrying over. 'Oh, thank heavens you've arrived . . . Something *terrible's* happened!'

Maria smiled and patted Pat's arm gently. It was plain to see the girl had been crying, that indeed she was in an excitable condition that on the least provocation might dive into hysteria.

'It's Keith,' Pat hurried on. 'That's the boy I was engaged to. I told you about him in my letters. I — '

'Miss *Black*!' exclaimed Mrs. Taylor, turning — and for a while Maria found herself in the midst of hasty introductions. She could see clearly that she had arrived at a moment when formalities were purely perfunctory, when everybody was thinking not of her but of the tragedy that had occurred.

The Superintendent came forward. 'I think I have all the details now,' he said briefly. 'Thank you. You'll all be summoned to the inquest. The ambulance will be here shortly — to convey the body to the mortuary, where the coroner can inspect it . . . The Sergeant will stay by the cellar door until the ambulance has been, then he will go too.' The Superintendent paused, looking at Maria. 'Good afternoon madam. I understand you are a friend of the family, not a relative?'

'Exactly so, Super,' Maria conceded, her eyes straying to the forgotten sandwiches and empty glasses on the big dining table.

'You were intending to attend this — er — party?'

'I was. If you wish to know why I didn't I would suggest you get in touch with the owner of a two-seater having the licence number HK-four seven one. That owner will confirm that I had a breakdown.'

'I hardly think that will be necessary, madam, but thank you just the same . . . You are most observant.'

Maria smiled. 'So I have been told. I also believe in taking precautions. I understand that a suicide has occurred: if you should have reason to doubt suicide you will naturally check the alibi of everybody in and out of the family. There you have mine.'

'Er — thank you,' the Superintendent acknowledged, and cleared his throat; then he turned and left the room.

There was silence, the deadly, stunned silence of inability to focus on the thing that had happened. It was broken by Ambrose Robinson muttering to himself.

''Oh that my grief were thoroughly weighed and my calamity laid in the balances together, for now it would be heavier than the sand of the sea . . . ' Job.'

Maria considered him with a concentrated gaze, then she gave a little cough. 'I — er — seem to have arrived at a terrible moment.'

'Yes . . . ' Mr. Taylor looked at her moodily from the other side of the room. 'Yes, you have, Miss Black. But I don't consider we would seem disrespectful if we made you welcome. Won't you please sit down?'

'I'll make you some tea,' Mrs. Taylor said, mechanically.

'Later,' Maria said, seating herself. 'I can see that you are all much distressed. I — '

'If nobody minds,' Madge Banning said, jumping up suddenly with a deathly pallor on her face, 'I'll be going home. I — I don't feel too well. 'Scuse me, won't you?'

She dashed from the room and swept

the door shut behind her She had hardly gone before Betty Andrews made a similar excuse. Ambrose Robinson, standing by the window, saw both girls flee down the street. He turned a gaunt face. The tragedy had left him hollow-eyed, his lips working spasmodically.

'I think, if you'll forgive me, that I'll follow the example of those two girls,' he said. 'I just couldn't stay here and watch them remove my boy . . . I must go home — be alone — offer a prayer for him . . . '

His voice tailed off as nobody spoke. He left the room Maria slanted an eye towards the window and watched his tall figure go down the pathway; then she looked back into the room. Mrs. Taylor shifted uneasily and said again that she ought to make some tea — but she did not move.

'Perhaps,' Maria said at last, 'I had better go on to my hotel and return here again later when you have had a chance to calm yourselves. This is hardly the time for entertaining a guest . . . '

'Hotel?' Pat repeated absently. 'What hotel? Aren't you staying with those friends of yours in Redford, Miss Black?'

'My friends left Redford long ago, my dear. However, I was determined to accept your kind invitation . . . So I made arrangements to stay a day or two in this part of the world, survey the local points of interest, and meantime put up at the Grand Hotel.'

'But you can stay here!' Mr. Taylor exclaimed. 'Why on earth didn't you tell us your friends had left?'

Maria smiled faintly. 'I am a most independent person, Mr. Taylor. I like hotels because if I do not approve of the service I can say so. One cannot in all courtesy deal with one's friends in that fashion.' Maria observed that her deliberate effort at conversation had somewhat broken the iron spell. 'I'm so sorry I was late. As you heard me tell the Superintendent, my car broke down. Do I understand that the young man you called Keith . . . committed suicide?'

'I was to marry him,' Pat said dully. 'I told you so in my letters. I wanted you to meet him — get an idea what you thought of him. He was such a queer chap in some things. I'd have been glad of an outside opinion; but naturally it doesn't matter any more.'

'Forgive me, but — what happened?' Maria asked.

Her question banished the last traces of the spell and all four Taylors started talking at once. They slowed up for a while as the ambulance arrived and the body was removed — the sergeant announcing that he was going with it — then the moment the front door had closed the talking resumed.

There was excitement in the voices now, each having his or her own version of what had happened. In the middle of it all Mrs. Taylor remembered her decision to make some tea — and did so. In due course Maria found herself with a cup of tea and a plateful of sandwiches on the table beside her.

'Extraordinary,' she admitted at last. 'Instead of coming to an engagement celebration I come to the suicide of the prospective bridegroom!'

'It's so illogical!' Mr. Taylor declared, his fists working. 'Why should any young man suddenly decide to hang himself in the middle of celebrating his engagement? No reason! No motive!'

'I think there was a motive,' Pat said suddenly, and she was very tense and hard-eyed. 'Sudden jealousy! It got him down!'

Her father looked astonished. 'Jealousy of what?'

'Remember you bringing up the matter of Billy Cranston and Cliff Evans? My two boyfriends?'

'Yes, but — Good heavens, Pat, that was only in fun! There was nothing in it.'

'Not to you, or me — not to any of us except Keith.' Pat gave a quick gesture. 'He tackled me twice about the other boys I know, and his jealousy of them amounted to rage. I do believe your mentioning them must have done some-thing to him and — and so he made up his mind to kill himself.'

'Doesn't sound very convincing to me, sis,' Gregory said, his lean, sallow face thoughtful.

'But, Greg, there couldn't have been any other motive,' Pat argued. 'Keith was healthy — or at any rate he seemed to be — and we were going to be married. He had everything to look forward to. Only his being overwhelmed by sudden jealousy could possibly account for his behaviour. It perhaps . . . unhinged his mind, or something. He was a bit funny sometimes,' Pat added, frowning reflectively.

'Funny?' Maria repeated.

Pat nodded. 'Yes. He was a prey to sudden moods. One moment he'd be on top of the world, and the next he'd be down in the doldrums. Sort of unstable.'

'Mmmm . . . ' Maria mused for a while and then she got to her feet. 'Well,' she said, 'the last thing I wish to do is to become involved in this tragic business, or foist myself upon you at such a time. I think it would be best if I went along to my hotel, carried out my programme of sightseeing in the next few days, and then return home. You can be sure you all have my deepest sympathy.'

Pat said urgently, 'Miss Black, you don't think I'm going to let you walk out like this, at such a time, do you? You're a wonderfully understanding person. I always used to come to you when I was in trouble at school: I want to do it now.'

'That was many years ago,' Maria answered, smiling. 'You have your mother and father. I am no longer your temporary guardian.'

'What Pat means, Miss Black, is that she trusts your judgment in some matters far more than she trusts mine — or her mother's.' As Mr. Taylor spoke there was still a baffled look on his round face. 'I can understand it,' he went on. 'You've had a wide experience of the world and of all sorts of people — especially young women. It isn't always the parents who are best fitted to understand their children.'

'But what is there I can do?' Maria spread her hands. 'I can only sympathize — nothing more. Pat, you surely don't expect me to try and guide your future life now that you've lost your intended husband?'

'It isn't that which worries me, Miss Black; it's the motive for Keith killing himself.'

'You just said it was jealousy.'

'Yes, I did, but . . . ' Pat reflected; then: 'That's what I think, and the more I think of it the more I believe Greg may be right in saying it's unconvincing. Perhaps there was another reason, but I'd never be able to find it. On the other hand, you might.'

'I?' Maria repeated. 'How?'

'You have odd ways of finding things out when you want to.' Pat sighed. 'What I'm trying to say is that Keith perhaps killed himself for a reason we none of us suspect, something perhaps that will never be revealed, not even at the inquest. For my part I'll never rest until I know why he did it.'

'Very well,' Maria said, 'if you feel I may be able to help you in any way I'll be only too happy. Sightseeing is hardly my exclusive idea of entertainment if there is a more human problem to tackle — '

'That's what I wanted you to say!' Pat cried in sudden eagerness. 'Stay here with us, at least till after the inquest. You can phone your hotel and cancel.'

Maria shrugged. 'If you wish.'

Mr. Taylor moved and managed a

smile. 'In future, Miss Black, I shall never believe the things I hear about headmistresses,' he said seriously. 'When Pat said she wanted you to come and join her celebration I thought she was crazy. Now I know otherwise . . . You stay here and make yourself at home. Your bags are in the car?'

'Yes. In the back.'

'I'll get them. And I think your car should be okay in the driveway. Unfortunately the garage is filled up with a broken-down car and I can't move it.'

It was eleven o'clock when Maria retired to the large bedroom at the front of the house that had been placed at her disposal. She had had a meal with the family at eight-thirty — consumed more as a token gesture than aught else — and had spent the rest of the evening making unsuccessful efforts to steer clear of the tragic topic with which they were all absorbed. The only diversion had come in the shape of a reporter who had rooted for facts, until he had been driven out by Maria's cold eyes and her demand that the bereavement of the people concerned should be respected.

Now she half lay in bed, pillows at her back, a bed-jacket about her shoulders. Her hair, released from the imprisoning moorings of the daytime, fell in waves and curls to well below her shoulders. Even at this age she had a mellow, aloof beauty all her own.

The book she was reading, Reik's *The Unknown Murderer*, did not appeal to her as much as usual. Her invariable half-hour of crime study, which for nearly twenty years she had pursued upon retiring, was clouded tonight by other considerations. Better than anybody in the house she knew that suicide by hanging could just as easily have been murder, it depending upon the skill of the murderer whether or not the fact was apparent to the investigators.

Maria frowned at a gentle tapping on the door 'Yes?' she called. 'Come in.'

Pat entered, a robe sashed in to her slender waist over her pyjamas. She closed the door softly, turned the key, and glided to the bedside. The table light caught her pale, straight features and the sheen in her dark hair.

'I'm glad you're not asleep, Miss Black,' she murmured.

Maria laid her book aside. 'I rarely succumb before midnight, my dear, and then I only permit myself seven hours. Bring up a chair.'

Pat did so and sat down. 'I thought I ought to tell you, Miss Black, that I had another reason for asking you to stay.'

'That much I had already assumed,' Maria commented. 'You really asked me to stay because you are not satisfied with the circumstances of Keith's suicide. You didn't creep in here just to sit and mope. You must have had a reason. What was it?'

'I've had an awful thought ever since Keith was found,' Pat said. 'Do you think that he might have been murdered?'

'Do you?' Maria asked directly.

'I don't know.' Pat rubbed a hand wearily across her forehead. 'I've got a sort of feeling — woman's intuition maybe.'

Maria laughed shortly. 'There isn't such a thing; take my word for it. A woman is a more sensitive animal than a man, yes, and for that reason only her imagination is usually keener. Intuition? No, my dear!' And she folded her heavy arms and waited.

'There was something about Keith's death that wasn't right,' Pat said slowly. 'I said jealousy made him do it because I couldn't think of anything else, but somehow I just don't believe that myself.' Pat leaned forward in sudden urgency, her fingers picking at the coverlet. 'Miss Black, you know a lot about crime and the reactions of criminals. Why don't you make some suggestion?'

'You expect me to say that I believe your fiancé was murdered?' Maria asked, astonished. 'But I haven't a shred of proof! I know hardly anything about his associations, his reactions, or if it comes to that his movements before he committed suicide ... Certainly I dabble in crime and at times I — hmm — have been able to help the police here and there, but only because I am untrammelled by regulations and can move freely, adopting the methods of investigation laid down by experts in their textbooks. In this particular case I cannot — nor would I — make comment. The police have been called and if there is any question of its being murder, you can rest assured they will find it.'

'But how can they? There's nothing to go on — except the rope with which Keith hanged himself.' Pat bit her lip. 'That won't tell them a thing!'

Maria smiled. 'On the contrary, my dear, it will tell them a great deal. It will depend on which way the rope fibres point.'

Pat frowned. 'What have rope fibres got to do with it?'

'That rope,' Maria said deliberately, beginning to enjoy herself, 'will now be in the hands of micro-analysts in the forensic laboratory. It will be microscopically examined. The rope will show if the weight was thrown on it suddenly — as in a genuine suicide — or if Keith was murdered and then hanged. The difference is between what is technically called 'slow strain' and 'two-way pull'.'

Pat grimaced. 'That's rather horrible!'

'No — just normal forensic technique.

But tell me, Pat, surely you don't think your fiancé was murdered? Who would want to do such a thing?'

'I've no idea. It's simply that I can't think he'd want to commit suicide, therefore the only answer is murder. I don't know why, or who, or anything about it. In fact nobody at the party could have done it because none of us left the room until it was found Keith had vanished.'

'I think you'd better try and keep your imagination in check, Pat,' Maria advised. 'You must be mistaken . . . In any case, if you have come here to ask me to do something, I just can't — not until I have all the details. The best thing I can do is attend the inquest and then let you know what I think.'

'Yes,' Pat agreed listlessly, rising and returning the chair beside the wall. 'I suppose that would be best. I'm sorry I bothered you at this hour, Miss Black.'

Maria's only response was an indulgent smile. She sat pondering for quite a time after the girl had left.

5

A day intervened before the inquest and Maria spent this day as far as she could outdoors, sharply aware that the death of Keith Robinson had left a hangover upon the Taylor family which had not yet been overcome. She did not refer to the matter any more than she could help, preferring to hear the questions and answers at the inquest before coming to a conclusion.

The inquest was held on the Friday morning in the local coroner's court, which on less judicial occasions served as an exhibition hall. Maria — since she was not a witness — seated herself amidst the spectators, most of them of the kind to whom anything morbid has a magnetic fascination. With her hands clamped on the chubby handle of her sunshade she sat upright and attentive.

Superintendent Haslow gave his evidence in a strictly formal tone. After meticulous care in regard to the time when he had viewed the body, he went on to the matter of the rope.

'I have forensic laboratory evidence, sir, which — in so far as the rope is concerned — eliminates all possibility of foul play,' he said. 'It would appear that the deceased stood on the solitary backless chair which was in the cellar, tied the clothes-rope about his neck, and the other end of the rope was secured to an iron staple driven into a beam which crosses the ceiling. Then he must have kicked the chair from under him and so hanged himself.'

Maria appeared to be asleep, her eyelids lowered. Aldyce, the expert from the forensic department, took up the story and went into a complicated explanation of 'slow strain' and 'two-way pull' for the benefit of the jury and the wonder of the public.

'As far as you, Mr. Aldyce, are concerned, there is no shadow of doubt that the sudden strain thrown upon the clothes-rope was quite normal for a suicide,' the coroner observed. 'But would it not be possible for the deceased to have been stood upon the chair by somebody else, have the rope fastened about his neck, and then have the chair moved from under him, thereby producing an identical effect?'

Aldyce admitted that this would be possible and added an apology that this was hardly his field. What point the coroner was trying to make was not clear. Dr. Standish came next and gave evidence to the effect that strangulation had been the cause of death, and then he went into detail concerning the abrasion marks on the neck. The coroner came back to his former point.

'Dr. Standish, as a medical man, do you believe it would be possible to tell if the deceased were dead — or maybe unconscious — *before* being hanged?'

'It would not be possible to tell,' Standish answered positively. 'If I may be permitted, I would like to quote a relevant statement by Hans Gross in his *Criminal Investigation* . . . ' The medico produced a slip of paper and read it aloud. ''A long line of medical jurisprudents has established that marks of strangulation inflicted on a living person are hardly, if at all, to be distinguished from those produced on a corpse, particularly if death be very recent'.'

'Thank you, Doctor,' the coroner said, who had hardly expected a quotation from the criminologist's 'Bible'. 'We are in the position, then, that death by hanging could either have been suicide or murder, and physically it wouldn't be possible to tell the difference.'

'That is so, sir.'

Maria rubbed the end of her long nose gently, then she became motionless again as Pat Taylor went through the hoops. The questions and answers came to Maria out of a great void.

' . . . and then, Miss Taylor, you called the attention of the gathering to the fact that Mr. Keith Robinson was not present?'

'Yes, sir, I did. I'd been talking to my two girl friends and the room was pretty full, all of us talking at once. Some point arose between my girl friends and I — I don't remember what it was now — and I wanted to ask Keith's opinion. Then I found he wasn't with us.'

'And when had you previously seen him? How long before?'

'About — er — about ten minutes perhaps. He had been talking to my father in an opposite corner by the doorway.'

'And your fiancé gave no hint that he intended leaving the room?'

'No hint whatever. I mentioned that he wasn't present and went to look for him. I couldn't find him; so Mr. Robinson — his father — went to look for him too, and he had no better luck. Finally we all started on a search. It was when we broke the cellar door down that we saw . . . the shadow of him hanging. Dad told us to stand back whilst he investigated.'

'And you did not hear a call for help or anything?'

'No. But I hardly think we would have over the noise going on in the room.'

'Can you think of any reason, Miss Taylor, why your fiancé should have wished to take his life? Had he ever given any kind of hint?'

'Never, sir,' Pat declared vehemently.

'He was rather a moody sort of chap, but he — '

'Just a moment, Miss Taylor. How — 'moody'?'

'Well, he . . . ' Pat hesitated. 'It's hard to explain. For one thing he had a furiously jealous nature — even to the extent of withholding my engagement ring until I as good as swore that I would have nothing more to do with two boy friends I know.'

'A strange proposal indeed. And did you do as he asked?'

'Partly. I didn't actually promise, because to me the thing seemed to be beyond all reason. I was willing to make allowances because I really loved him — and after all none of us is perfect.'

'Besides his jealousy, was there any other facet of his nature which you considered peculiar?'

'Yes. He would act sometimes as though he had not heard what I'd said and start instead upon some observation of his own — quite possibly a matter which neither of us had mentioned. Then at other times he would become desperately depressed, but it changed so quickly to genial good-nature that I tried not to notice it too much.'

'In other words, he was erratic in temperament?'

'Very,' Pat agreed.

Maria opened her eyes. She considered the smoky ceiling, saw the vulture-like Ambrose Robinson taking Pat's place. She closed her eyes again.

'My son was wayward!' Ambrose Robinson declared, and then went on to outline events in much the same words as Pat. 'I tried to direct his path in the way it should go. I tried to make him upright and God-fearing, as I am, but he preferred the sins of this world — '

'Quite so, Mr. Robinson, but that is hardly what we wish to know. We are trying to establish, if possible, the reason for your son's behaviour. Do you confirm that he had a jealous disposition?'

'Certainly he had — and he was up in spirits one minute and down in the dumps the next. It was because he was so unsettled in mind and actions that I tried to keep him beside me. I had the idea of taking him into my business eventually.'

'You are an ironmonger and locksmith, Mr. Robinson?'

'Yes — an honest, upright trade. My son preferred to work at the railway station as a costings clerk. I didn't approve but he was at an age to please himself.'

'Did you and your son live amicably together, or was there friction?'

'There was friction — all the time.'

'Why?'

'Because I believe in the teachings of the Bible and my son did not. That was why I say he chose the world and its wickedness. 'The righteous shall hold on his way, and he that hath clean hands shall be stronger and stronger . . . ' So sayeth Job.'

There was something like a titter in the court until an usher stopped it.

'Did you approve of your son becoming engaged to Miss Taylor, Mr. Robinson?'

'I did not!' Ambrose Robinson snapped, the point of his chin and the end of his nose nearly touching in the aggressiveness of his expression. 'On the evening he became engaged he came home intoxicated. Never before until that moment had the disgusting odour of drink defiled my home — and then it came from the lips of my son! And, much as I regret to say it, from my potential daughter-in-law too.'

'You surely do not infer that your son and Miss Taylor were the worse for drink?'

In cold disdain Ambrose Robinson gave the facts. Maria was no longer apparently asleep. Her eyes were wide open and her interest aroused.

'So, then, your son relapsed into a stupor because of a glass of wine? Had he never had intoxicant before?'

'Not to my knowledge. I have already said that the taint of drink had never been in my home until then.'

'Do you think it likely that your disapproval of his engagement led him to commit the act he did?'

'I just don't know,' Ambrose Robinson replied. 'But if he did commit the act I think he did it as atonement for the sin he contemplated performing.'

'Sin?' the coroner repeated sharply. 'Do you mean you think marriage is a sin?'

'As far as my son was concerned, yes. I warned him that to marry a woman who had insisted he drink wine could only end in disaster. I can only think that at the last moment, during the celebration, he realized the folly of what he was intending to do, and decided to take his life. That too was a mortal sin in the eyes of the law, yes — but it was also a magnificent atonement.'

Maria's eyes followed the gaunt locksmith as he returned to his seat. Her lips tightened and the clasp she had upon the chubby handle of her sunshade became firmer.

Mr. Taylor came next with his story of the discovery of the body. He went into detail as to how they had all seen the shadow of it hanging on the wall. He explained how he had taken charge of the proceedings and cut the body down.

'Apparently, Mr. Taylor, you were the last person to be seen talking to the deceased. He did not tell you anything, either, which might have given a hint as to his intentions?'

'He certainly didn't,' Mr. Taylor answered,

shrugging. 'As for our conversation, it was purely general — and partly concerned with his future. As far as I could tell he was in the best of spirits.'

'I see. About this wine that the young man had on the night of his engagement. Was it ordinary wine?'

'Yes. Good brand of port. We all had some — that is, young Keith, my daughter, my son, and my wife. And myself of course. Probably the wine and the hot weather and the excitement of being engaged were too much for him all at once.'

Pause. 'At the party on the night of the tragedy you all had lemonade, did you not?'

'Yes. That was my daughter's idea, to prevent Keith being overcome as he had on the previous occasion.'

'It would seem, since he used the rope and the chair in the cellar, that he must have known beforehand that they were there. Can you account for that? Had he ever seen the basement before?'

Mr. Taylor nodded promptly. 'Yes, of course. On the evening I went down to get the wine. He accompanied me into the cellar. As a matter of fact I asked him to so that I could have him to myself for a moment or two and tell him that I thoroughly approved of him as a potential son-in-law. I firmly believed that my daughter had made an excellent choice.'

'Then you were not concerned over the young man s seemingly erratic nature?'

'Not a bit. Come to that, all of us are a bit touchy in some way. I didn't think Keith was worse in that respect than anybody else. Anyway, Pat was satisfied and that was all that mattered to me.'

Thereafter Mr. Taylor had little more to impart. He was replaced by his wife, and then Gregory, and finally the two girls who had been present — but they had little of material value to add. In fact it looked to Maria as though the proceedings were slowing to a halt, when, to her surprise — and evidently to the surprise of those involved as well — a trim little man with a birdlike face was called. The coroner spoke slowly.

'Throughout this inquest,' he said, looking at the jury, 'we have sought to establish the condition of the deceased's mind at the time of death. We have heard from the various witnesses that he was of erratic temperament, which suggests he had a mental instability. I would ask you to pay close attention to the evidence now about to be placed before you . . . '

Maria sat motionless, absorbed.

'Be so good as to tell the court your name and profession, Doctor,' the coroner instructed.

The birdlike man said: 'I am Dr. Adam Cherwood, resident acting superintendent of the Sunbeam Home of Rest in Banley, Surrey.'

'Is it not a fact, Doctor, that the records of the Sunbeam Home of Rest show that on August 10, twenty years ago, a patient was admitted to that institution and there died on July 5, three years later? A patient by the name of Evelyn Robinson? The mother of the deceased?'

'Yes, sir, that is correct.'

'I protest!' Ambrose Robinson cried, jumping up. 'What gives you the right to drag the name of my dear wife into this — ?'

'Mr. Robinson,' the coroner intervened patiently, 'I can well understand your feelings, but you must remember that we have got to establish beyond doubt the state of your son's mind when he committed suicide. The police, working on the possible hypothesis of hereditary insanity, investigated your son's parentage on the mother's side — '

' 'God hath delivered me to the ungodly and turned me over to the hands of the wicked!' ' Ambrose Robinson stormed.

'Silence!' commanded an usher. 'Be seated!'

Ambrose Robinson sat down slowly and buried his face in his hands. The deliberate voice of Dr. Cherwood continued:

'Yes, Evelyn Robinson died in the Sunbeam Home of Rest, of a heart attack.'

'Prior to that, Doctor, what was her condition?'

'Towards the end — *dementia praecox*.'

Maria relaxed against the back of her chair and closed her eyes again. The coroner began his summing up.

' . . . and so, gentlemen of the jury,' he concluded, 'you now have the facts before you and you have heard the evidence of the various witnesses. It is for you to use your common sense and decide whether the deceased took his own life in a moment of mental unbalance — a quite possible occurrence in view of his mother's unhappy condition — or whether he was the victim of some cleverly organized foul play, for which you must remember there is not one shred of evidence . . . So, gentlemen of the jury . . . '

The result was a foregone conclusion. At 11.45, an hour and fifteen minutes since the start of the inquest, the jury returned a verdict of 'Suicide whilst of unsound mind'.

Maria was waiting outside the building, a massive, thoughtful figure considering Redford's main street, when at length the Taylors, Ambrose Robinson, and Pat's two girl friends came in view.

Pat broke free of the party. 'I suppose you heard everything, Miss Black? What did you think?'

'Since the jury have returned their verdict upon the evidence supplied, what can my opinion matter?'

'It can matter a great deal,' Pat declared.

Maria glanced towards the girl's mother and father. 'I have a suggestion to make,' Maria said. 'Come to lunch with me, Pat, away from home for a change, and have a little chat. I'll arrange it . . . ' She did not give the girl a chance to comment. Instead she turned to the Taylors and Ambrose Robinson with a murmured condolence for their ordeal.

'They had no right to drag in that business about my poor wife!' Ambrose Robinson declared angrily. 'Is it not enough for a man to be held up in public as the father of a suicide without also being pointed to as the husband of a woman who was a — a . . . '

'Let it pass, Mr. Robinson,' Maria interposed gently, patting his arm. 'You must remember that the police have a job to do. And they did it thoroughly.'

'Won't you come and have some lunch with us, Ambrose?' Mrs. Taylor insisted.

'You don't want to go home at a time like this. Besides, though I hate bringing it up, there is the matter of the funeral to discuss. It's got to be done.'

'I should do just that, Mr. Robinson,' Maria advised. 'Without any disrespect to the dead — life goes on, you know. For my part I think I'll take Pat to lunch in town here. Maybe I can give her a bit of encouragement for the future.'

'That's a mighty good idea!' Mr. Taylor declared.

Maria smiled, then with a nod of farewell she turned and motioned the waiting Pat into the Austin Seven. In a moment or two they were progressing up the street.

'Which restaurant do you suggest?' Maria asked. 'That is, apart from the one in which you are employed: the manager might even expect you to start work! He can wait until the funeral is over. You are entitled to have time to recover, same as anybody else . . . '

'Try Maddison's; they're a bit further along the street past our place,' Pat said, and she directed the way until Maria drew up outside a small but spotlessly clean restaurant with net curtains drawn taut across the windows.

She locked up the car and then she and Pat went inside and found a corner table more or less isolated. Maria gave the order, taking no refusal as Pat listlessly pondered whether she could have anything or not.

'I never knew Keith's mother was . . . insane,' Pat whispered, a glint of tears in her dark eyes. 'It was a terrible shock to me to hear it — but at least it made a lot of things understandable at the same time.'

'Such as?'

'Why, Keith's queer little ways — that moodiness I told you about; his disinterest in important things, his exaggeration of trifles. Above all, his sudden decision to commit suicide. Perhaps — perhaps it was as well. I mean, any children we might have had . . . '

As Maria remained silent, the girl added: 'I think that must have been why old Mr. Robinson so strongly disapproved. He didn't wish to state the real reason and so he picked on the absurd angle of drink to try and break things up.'

The waitress arrived and set out the meal, together with the pot of tea and cups on which Maria had insisted.

'One thing I refuse to tolerate is lack of tea with a meal,' she said. 'Here you are, my dear — and do you mind if I ask you a rather personal question?'

'What is it?'

'In the course of your attachment to that unfortunate young man, did he write you any letters of — hmm! — endearment?'

'Several.' Pat stirred her tea and sipped it. 'I've a whole packet of them at home.'

'Were they eloquent? Amorous?'

'Tremendously so. Certainly there was nothing wrong with Keith when he wrote them — In fact I have one with me. Care to see it?'

'Very much.'

Pat snapped open her handbag, rummaged for a moment, and then handed a letter over. 'It was the last one he sent me, the day before he gave me the ring and we became officially engaged.'

Maria took the letter and read it aloud, but with her voice modulated so that it did not travel beyond their immediate table.

'My darling Pat, I am hoping with an inordinate zest that nothing will detain you beyond the appointed hour tomorrow evening. Deep within me is something of profound moment, which I must impart to you — a great surprise — and were you to be late my horizon would be as limited as the outlook of an amoeba. No yardstick can measure the height nor plumb the phenomenal depth of the regard I have for you. Make it six as usual tomorrow, Keith.'

Pat met Maria's ice-blue eyes across the table. 'I know it sounds a bit silly, but he always wrote like that.'

'You are sure?' Maria questioned sharply.

'Certainly! You can see the other letters if you wish. It was just his funny way of putting things.'

Maria handed the letter back. 'I don't

want to sound brutal, my dear, but this letter — without there being any need of seeing the others he wrote — amply justifies the hypothesis that he was mentally deranged. In fact had I seen one of them beforehand I would have told you as much, and warned you.'

'You mean — you mean you can tell from a letter?'

'Hardly!' Maria's smile was wintry for a moment. 'You are fully aware that I study criminology. It is an acknowledged fact that a person afflicted with a mental aberration will often use words of extraordinary formation and unusual length. It is also true that the statements are meaningless in some respects — as those are. Observe the absurd symbolism of the 'the limited horizon of an amoeba' and then the ludicrous reference to a 'yardstick' for 'measuring regard'. Compare that with the final perfectly normal 'Make it six as usual tomorrow' and you can trace the mental processes behind the letter.'

'Great heavens!' Pat looked at the letter stupidly and then slowly folded it. 'Such a thing never even dawned on me. And he wrote piles of them, and all in the same vein! I thought it was literary inclination.'

'Hardly.' Maria took a little more tea and something to eat before she resumed. Then: 'I asked for a letter to satisfy myself that mental instability might be at the back of everything. I am now satisfied. Keith was not normal, though he was not, of course, certifiable. And that being so I do not believe he did commit suicide. I think that he was murdered. I've a reason for thinking so apart from what I've told you.'

'But that's impossible! You heard the evidence in court, and the verdict. There's not the slightest proof of foul play.'

'Not on the surface perhaps, but consider something.' Maria's eyes narrowed. 'According to the evidence Keith had only seen the cellar once, when he went with your father to get the wine. They exchanged confidences — so your father said. What matters is that Keith had only a chance to glance about the cellar when he perhaps noticed that there was a hard, tough rope, a backless chair, and a staple in the beam from which he was later found hanging. I do not really believe that in those few moments he would have had the time to weigh things up so completely . . . And further, since he did not enter the cellar again until he was found hanging, how was he to know the chair and rope would still be there?'

'I just can't imagine how he could have been murdered,' Pat mused. 'Every one of us was in the drawing room — and none of us left it except Keith . . . And don't forget that the cellar door was locked on the inside. It's the only way in and out of the cellar, so how could a murderer have committed the crime?'

'There are of course ways of turning a key from the outside of a door,' Maria commented, 'but in this instance they may not be applicable. That points instead to an ingeniously devised crime, so skilfully done that even the police were fooled.'

Pat looked troubled. 'I've just had an awful thought! I wondered for a moment if Mr. Robinson could have had anything to do with it. For one thing he's a locksmith, and for another he might have wanted to stop the marriage by violent means. Being a locksmith would give him a knowledge of wangling keys.'

'Interesting,' Maria admitted, then she shrugged. 'However, the locked door is, in terms of sequence, at the end of the problem — not the beginning. So let us get down to essentials . . . and I'd remind you that your meal is getting cold.'

Swayed by the majestic spell of Maria's presence, Pat behaved as though she were once more a pupil in the dining hall at Roseway. She ate her meal, and felt better for it.

'I am in an awkward position,' Maria said at last, looking across at Pat. 'My knowledge of crime leads me to believe that murder has been done, and if I were to follow my own inclinations I would root out the whole business from top to bottom . . . But your parents and brother could rightly object if I started exploring in your home: they could even have the law restrain me if they wished. The coroner's verdict has been given and there, technically, barring some very startling new evidence — such as a confession of murder — the matter rests.'

'Is there anything to stop you telling the police what you have told me, and have them investigate?' Pat asked.

'No, there is nothing to stop that — only I don't think they would listen very attentively to the theories of a middle-aged headmistress.'

'But you're not just that, Miss Black! You're a detective — and you've proved it on many occasions. After all, don't the papers reverse your names and call you 'Black Maria'?'

Maria chuckled. 'I invented that name myself, Pat. It struck me as quite unique . . . However, whether the police have heard of my activities or not, I still do not think they would take kindly to my theory. You see, I am — hmm — somewhat unorthodox in my methods. I select what I think is a weak point in the chain of evidence and then I make it my business to press home my advantage. It does not always work — but in certain cases I've been successful. If anything is to be discovered about this particular homicidal crime, then I am certainly the only one who can do it.'

'And, of course, the starting point would have to be at home,' Pat commented. 'Yes, I can see how difficult it might be . . . I don't know how Mother, Dad and Greg would react. Personally, I don't think Mother and Dad would mind for a moment — but Greg certainly would.'

'Yes,' Maria nodded. 'Since he is a legal man he would probably get to work to set me moving about my business . . . Pat, tell me something. Do you really want me to try and get to the bottom of this business? Have you realized what unhappy consequences there might be for you if the criminal happened to be somebody in your own family?'

Pat laughed. 'If that is the only risk there is I'll take it. Naturally, it couldn't be Mother, Father, or Greg . . . And I think I have an answer to our problem,' she went on eagerly. 'I'll take the rest of this week off from business and you must stay with us. With the exception of Sunday, Greg. and Dad will be out at business. The only other time they'll be at home is for the funeral . . . What I mean is, Mother will be the only one we need to worry about, and she'll see this business as I see it — and if there is more evidence to be found, then it must be found. All of which means you can poke about as you wish.'

'Excellent!' Maria declared, beaming. 'And if by any chance we should be caught in the midst of our activities I have not the least doubt that I shall be equal to the occasion . . . ' She glanced about the now crowded café and raised an imperious hand. 'Waitress! My check, if you please . . . '

6

It was shortly after two o'clock when Maria and Pat returned to the quiet house in Cypress Avenue. Only Mrs. Taylor was present, in the midst of washing up a pile of dinner crocks. She looked round from the sink, her face warm and smudged, as Maria and Pat looked in on her.

'Greg and Harry have gone to business,' Mrs. Taylor explained, blowing a wisp of blonde hair out of her eye. 'They lost all this morning, you know . . . Oh, did you have lunch?'

'Yes, indeed,' Maria agreed, removing her hat. 'We conversed at length. I need hardly say that this morning's revelations upset Pat quite a deal.'

'They upset me, too!' For a moment the oozing good-humour went from Mrs. Taylor's chubby face. 'To think that that lad was *crazy*! Or as good as, anyway. It never so much as occurred to me . . . If you ask me, Pat had a merciful escape. A thing like that might have led into just anything! I told Ambrose as much, too. Upbraided him, I did!'

'And what did he say to that?' Maria asked.

'Something about if Pat would have Keith, what use was there in arguing. Then he recited a lot of Scripture . . . '

'I said to Miss Black that I'd escaped a lot,' Pat muttered; then hastily she added: 'Mum, I've asked Miss Black to stay on for a few days now she's here. It's all right, isn't it?'

'Of course!' Mrs. Taylor smiled. 'You need somebody like Miss Black to keep you from thinking too much about yourself.'

The thing was done. Maria was in the house — to stay for as long as she deemed expedient. She met Pat's eager expression with a complacent smile . . . Turning, she went upstairs to freshen up. When she came down again she found that Pat was lingering in the hall.

'Couldn't be better,' Pat said, her voice eager. 'Mother's gone shopping. We've got the place to ourselves if you want to do any . . . snooping.'

'Hmm — quite!' Maria came forward from the foot of the stairs. 'I think to commence with that we should take a look at the cellar.'

Pat nodded and moved to the cellar door. She turned the key and the door swung open. Maria paused and looked at the lock carefully. It had been screwed back in position again.

'Greg did it,' Pat explained, catching Maria's eye. 'No use leaving the lock half off, was it?'

'No,' Maria agreed. 'No indeed . . . ' She moved to the top of the curving wooden stairway and stood gazing down it after Pat had switched on the light. 'As I understand it, Pat, you saw the shadow of Keith's hanging body on the left-hand wall there?'

'That's right, Miss Black. We all did.'

'The shadow being cast by the light bulb which, at the moment, is out of sight behind that wall at the stairway base?'

'That's it,' Pat confirmed.

Maria's hand strayed to the slender

thread of gold watch-chain depending down her ample bosom. Pat half smiled to herself as she noticed the habit. Quite unwittingly Maria always revealed when she was thinking hard by twisting the watch-chain in and out of her fingers.

'Was this shadow life-size?' Maria questioned, after a moment or two. 'That is to say, had it approximately the same dimensions as Keith?'

Pat reflected. 'Well, yes; I think it had. Naturally, I got such a shock that I didn't look at it beyond a second or two.'

'I see. Incidentally, I am somewhat at a disadvantage. I never saw Keith, remember. How big was he?'

'He was on the short side — at least an inch less than I. I'd say he was five feet four and of very slender build.'

'Mmmm . . . ' Maria transferred her hand from the watch-chain to what appeared to be a fountain pen in the bosom of her dress. It proved to be a small torch, the narrow beam from which she directed onto the back of the door — the side that faced the cellar. For a while the light hovered upon the replaced key-lock.

'Your father and brother smashed the door open, did they not?' she asked absently.

'That's right, and the key was in the inside — *this* side. The only answer to that is that Keith must have taken the key out of the outside of the lock and then locked himself in here. Why, I can't imagine.'

'At the moment, neither can I,' Maria responded.

She returned the torch to her dress and went down the curving wooden stairs until she came into the glare of the electric light. Thoughtfully she looked about her upon the whitewashed walls and ceiling.

From her present position the base of the curved staircase was on her left. A couple of yards from it, directly over her head, was the electric light, hanging on a length of flex about a foot long, the flex imbedded into the plaster ceiling with a conventional porcelain cap.

To her right was the empty, rusty fireplace, the brickwork above it coming forward about two feet from the wall to form a chimneybreast. A foot away from the electric light fixture was a thick beam, whitewashed, going the length of the ceiling, the fireplace at one end of it and the opposite wall of the cellar at the other.

Standing beside the fireplace was the backless chair that had figured in the suicide. Maria turned. Behind her was the old-fashioned fire-heated washing copper, a wringer, and a galvanized tub.

'What is in there?' she asked, and nodded to the doorway beside the copper.

'That? It used to be the coal cellar. There's a grating in its roof that leads to the back garden. When we came to live here Dad said he didn't like the idea of climbing up and down steps to get coal, so he had an outhouse built next to the garage. That door was then screwed up — just in case it made a handy entrance for a burglar. It's still screwed, as you can see for yourself.'

Maria walked over and examined it. There were six big screws driven into the sides of the door, the heads of which were flaky with rust. It was obvious they had not been disturbed since the day they had been driven home.

'Most interesting,' she commented. 'In which case, except for the chimney, there is no other means of entrance or exit except by the hall door.'

'Chimney?' Pat repeated. 'You can't include that, Miss Black. It's only narrow. A child might get up and down it, but nobody else.'

Maria strolled over until she was under the central ceiling beam. She stood gazing up at it, the heavy staple on which the body had been hanging being plainly visible.

'Does that staple have any ordinary use?' she enquired.

'No. It was there when we came, seven years ago. I should imagine that it was once used to hang bacon or ham on.'

Maria drew forward the backless chair, stood on it, and then inspected the staple more closely in the bright electric light. It was rusty, but foundationally very strong. She estimated, by pulling on it, that it could easily hold one slightly-built man. It had been driven into the beam at a slightly upwardly tilting angle. At the base, where it entered the beam, the rust had been rubbed away by the friction of the death-rope.

'Isn't much to tell from that staple, Miss Black, is there?' Pat asked, craning back her head and staring upwards.

'I'm afraid not,' Maria confessed. 'I notice that there are traces of fibre from the clothes-rope which have caught in the rough surface of the wood — but as far as I am concerned they have no significance.'

'I suppose we're not making a mistake?' Pat asked. 'Are you *sure* that Keith wouldn't be able to get a knowledge of this cellar and its contents by just glancing round once? After all, the forensic laboratory experts did say that the rope strands proved a sudden stress had been placed on the rope, which matches up with a suicide.'

'I would also remind you, my dear, that the forensic expert admitted that it would be possible for Keith to have been stood on this chair by somebody else, have the rope fastened about his neck, and then have the chair kicked from under him.'

Pat became silent, her expression troubled. Maria remained on the chair, unconsciously resembling a political agitator as she raised a finger to emphasize a further point.

'We must also consider the possibility, Pat, that the murderer could have known of the effect of 'slow strain' and 'two-way pull' and therefore arranged matters to look like a genuine suicide — even to overturning this chair in the manner *of* a suicide. We do not know that *Keith* knocked this chair over, the murderer could also have done it . . . ' Maria stopped and narrowed her eyes. 'Upon my word, we face a problem of remarkable ingenuity. Not a clue — not a trace. Whoever did this was, to say the least of it, competent.'

Pat nodded slowly. 'And the cellar door locked on the inside and all of us in the room upstairs when it must have happened. It couldn't have been murder, Miss Black. It's impossible!'

'In my experience, Pat, a lot of things could not have been — but they were, when I came to look more closely, as I must in this instance . . . '

Maria got down from the chair She walked over to the rusty old fire grate and studied it carefully. Pat joined her and gazed, too, but she saw nothing except a fall of powdery soot and the empty bars corroding with rust.

'I suppose,' Maria asked, 'this fireplace is not used?'

'It's never been used since we came,' Pat answered.

'That's interesting. I wonder how that got there . . . '

Maria pointed to greyish spots amidst the soot on the bars at the bottom of the grate. Pat moved closer and gave a little start of surprise.

'Why, it's candle-grease!'

'Candle-grease in a grate which is never used? That, to say the least of it, is unique.'

Pat shrugged. 'I don't suppose there's anything so mysterious about it, really. I expect that at some time when Dad or Greg or Mum came down here the light bulb fused — so they got a candle and stuck it in the grate while a new bulb was fitted.'

'In which case there should be traces of candle-fat on the floor,' Maria said. 'Suppose we see if there are . . . ?'

She and Pat began a careful search in the brightness of the electric light, but there was no trace of candle-grease anywhere else. Finally Maria returned to the grate and stood pondering it.

'If you came down here with a candle and wished to put it somewhere while you replaced a light bulb, would you stick it in the grate? The thick bars would cast a shadow across the cellar, for one thing. For another, there would be no reason for care in regard to the candle-grease, as there would be over a carpet. Fat dropping on this concrete just wouldn't matter . . . I think you would place the candle on the best vantage point — possibly the flat top of the copper.'

Pat looked across at it and nodded.

'Yes, I suppose I would. I was just wondering if the candle were in a candlestick, which prevented grease on the floor — but it just couldn't have been or grease wouldn't be in the grate.'

'And quite a lot of it has been splashed

there,' Maria said, looking at the spots again. 'And recently, too! Despite the sooty dust which has descended it has not entirely blackened these spots over.'

Leaning forward, Maria peered up into the black emptiness of the chimney. Her fountain-pen torch did not cast a beam strong enough to go beyond the first few layers of bricks — but she did see enough to satisfy her that no human being could possibly go up and down that narrow flue. As she withdrew she made a mental note to return later with the more powerful torch she carried in her luggage — chiefly in case of a car breakdown in the night.

'There's something else to be thought of, Miss Black,' Pat said. 'If Keith was murdered, why on earth didn't he put up a struggle? Surely he wouldn't take it tamely?'

'Nobody takes tamely to the idea of being killed,' Maria observed dryly. 'But how do you know he *didn't* struggle?'

'I don't. I'm just — suggesting. There are no signs of there having been a fight or anything.'

'In a practically empty cellar with a concrete floor?' Maria shook her head. 'My dear, you expect impossibilities! If Keith struggled at all there were certainly no traces of it on his person. No bruises — no anything, according to the evidence. Only the mark of the clothes-rope . . . ' She paused, then: 'I think we are hastening ahead of the immediate problem, Pat. Up to now we have only two pointers in this whole strange business — the rest is merely airy assumption that is of no use whatever. The two pointers are: (a) That Keith did not have time to decide that this cellar was a suitable spot in which to commit suicide; and (b) candle-grease in a grate never used for a fire. Upon those two aspects I shall concentrate . . . And now I think we might return to the upper regions.'

Pat nodded. Maria went up the wooden staircase slowly and paused when she reached the top. From this elevated angle she considered the aspect below.

'Six of the steps are in view from the top here, and the remaining five at the base are out of sight because they

116

turn in a curve into the cellar . . . Hmmm.'
Maria began stroking her watch-chain.
'Tell me, Pat, what kind of a shadow was
it you saw? Was the shadow a clear-cut
one, or was it hazy?'

'Far as I remember it looked just the
same as any shadow looks,' Pat said.

'Think hard! This may be of great
importance.'

'The trouble is I didn't get the chance
to see it for long,' Pat said. 'I just don't
remember how it looked. It was simply a
shadow — but somehow I seem to have
the lingering idea that it was . . . hazy.'

'Hazy? Right,' Maria said, and after
giving a final look round she moved on
into the hall. Pat followed her, switched
off the cellar light, and closed the door.

'Might as well go in the drawing room,'
Pat said, motioning, and with a nod
Maria preceded her, finally selecting an
armchair and sitting down.

Pat looked at her inquiringly. 'Well,
Miss Black, what happens next?'

'I think, Pat, that I should spend the
evening at the cinema,' Maria answered,
beaming.

'The cinema? But what about the candle grease, and — and Keith, and — ' Then Pat stopped before a dramatically raised hand.

'My dear, when you reach my age you will discover that there is no art so necessary as detachment. I make a rule never to work my brain to no purpose. I have gathered all I can, or indeed intend to gather, for one day. Those two points I mentioned must tell, and they will only do that by my detaching my mind from them . . . Have you a local paper? What films are showing?'

Deeply puzzled, Pat hunted round for a newspaper, and in the process she seemed to collect endless thriller and detective magazines of the more garish American variety. Maria got to her feet and looked at the covers on some of the monthlies as Pat tossed them on one side.

'Hmm!' Maria cleared her throat. 'Amazing! *No Flowers for My Grave* . . . *A Body Lies A-rotting* — Most unpleasant! *Death Has no* — hmm — *Stink*! Extraordinary. Are you responsible for this collection of — er

— shockers, Pat?'

'No — it's all Greg's stuff. He reads every thriller under the sun. At the moment he's collecting a serial — *Death in Deep Water*. I read 'em myself sometimes, but I'm not too interested. If you think this pile is anything you should see the back room!' Pat reached behind a cushion on the chesterfield. 'Ah! Here's last night's paper . . . Now, let's see.'

'Perhaps,' Maria murmured, taking the paper from her gently, 'I might be a better judge of my own tastes . . . What have we now? Ah, this looks promising — *Fiancé to a Killer*. At the Rialto. Where is the Rialto?'

'Oh, it's one of the best places in town — large car park attached, too.'

'Splendid! And the show is continuous from six. Yes, that will do admirably.'

Pat sighed. 'I'd go myself if it were not for what's happened. But since there's not even been the funeral yet I could hardly go . . . could I?'

'No,' Maria said, and put an end to the girl's wavering. 'As far as I am concerned it does not make the least difference,

119

since I did not even know Keith, nor shall I be a mourner at his funeral . . . '

Except for a drink of tea when Mrs. Taylor returned from her shopping expedition, Maria did not trouble with a meal. Instead she left the house towards five and drove into town in her Austin Seven. She enjoyed a comfortable tea in Maddison's Café and then continued her journey to the Rialto, arriving in ample time for the commencement of the performance.

She saw the show through from beginning to end, her hands damped on her sunshade handle and her eyes fixed on the screen. Even so, she had little idea what the films were about. To her they were just movements, voices, and at times noisy background music. Her exact reason for sitting here in the back stalls was that she could have soft lighting and comparative peace, neither of which she would have been able to find at the Taylor home. The mechanical noise of the films she hardly noticed: she had the gift of detaching herself from her surroundings.

'The most important thing is that

nobody saw the body,' she mused to herself, as she finally tracked her way through the ornate foyer at quarter past nine. 'Just the shadow of a body — which gives rise to another point . . . '

She stopped, staring into space, puzzling something out. An usherette in revealingly tight wine-coloured pants glided up to her.

'Main exit straight ahead, madam. Car park exit on the left. Good night, madam.'

Maria frowned at the interruption to her train of thought, then went on her way leftwards. 'The point is,' she told herself, 'if the shadow of the body were there to commence with, why didn't Keith see it and come quickly out of the cellar? Mmm . . . yes, most intriguing possibility.'

Entering her car, she drove back at a leisurely speed towards the Taylor home. By the time she had brought the car to a standstill in the driveway of the house a whole mass of hazy questions — and in some cases their answers — had taken shape in her mind. Her few hours in the depths of the cinema had been well spent.

Pat admitted her into the house. When Maria came into the drawing room she found the entire family present. Mr. Taylor was on the chesterfield under the window, reading the newspaper. At the other side of the room Gregory was deep in a crime magazine, his hair as polished and flawlessly exact as ever. Mrs. Taylor had been at the table, sewing, but she lowered it to her lap as Maria entered.

'Did you enjoy your film?' she asked.

'I found the outing most stimulating,' Maria responded, settling in an armchair and interlacing her fingers.

Gregory Taylor lowered his magazine and looked at Maria from the corner. 'Did you find it as stimulating as hunting a criminal in real life, Miss Black?' he asked.

Maria smiled urbanely. 'There is nothing quite so stimulating as real life, Mr. Taylor ... Especially so when hunting a criminal.'

Gregory got to his feet and crossed to the empty fireplace. He leaned against the mantel, his light grey eyes summing Maria up.

'Miss Black, Mother and Pat were saying at teatime that you have decided to stay with us for a few days — to help Pat over the shock?'

'That is my intention,' Maria assented. 'However, since I have no wish to be in the way I am hoping that Pat and I will be able to get out a little together in this lovely weather. But for what might have been said Pat would have come with me to the cinema tonight.'

Gregory gave a cold smile. 'Why not say outright that you think Keith was murdered, and that you're staying here to see if you can't find out how it was done?'

Mr. Taylor stirred and peered over his reading glasses. 'Murdered? What in the world are you talking about, Greg?'

Gregory Taylor took a cigarette from his case and examined it carefully before lighting it.

'Am I right, Miss Black?' he asked, and met the impact of her frosty blue eyes. 'You see,' Gregory went on pensively, 'I know your reputation. I probably know more about it than Pat, if it comes to that, even though she went to your college.'

'Most interesting,' Maria commented, and waited.

Gregory continued: 'I am interested in crime, criminals, detectives, mysteries, and the whole caboosh. I have newspaper cuttings of the cases in which you personally lent a hand. That affair in New York for one, the cinema murder in Langhorn for another . . . As Black Maria you seem to have earned quite a reputation for yourself.'

Maria remained silent. She could not determine whether Gregory was going to shake her hand or burst into a rage.

'So,' Gregory went on, whilst his mother, father, and sister listened in astonishment, 'I asked myself at teatime — what does Miss Black, an active, intelligent woman with many interests, want to stay with us for? To comfort Pat? Hardly! Pat is already recovered: she only loved Keith Robinson because of his looks, anyway. There was certainly no soul-mate stuff about it — '

'I resent that!' Pat broke in angrily. 'I

really loved Keith!'

'No, you didn't, sis — not really. You were perhaps sorry for him because he lived an uncomfortable life with his father. Or maybe you liked Keith's company. But I still think it was his handsome looks, and nothing more. Had you really loved him you would have been much more grief-stricken upon his death . . . '

Gregory knocked the ash from his cigarette into the grate. 'You are interested in only two things. Miss Black — your college and the activities of criminals. It couldn't be your college, since the summer vacation has started — '

'Incorrect,' Maria murmured. 'I have my deputy controlling things. My visit here was specially made. But continue.'

'It couldn't be your college, so it must be crime. You heard the inquest and then decided to stay on. Because the verdict did not satisfy you . . . Am I right?'

'Your legal training, young man, is more than obvious,' Maria observed blandly. 'But I am under no obligation to answer your question.'

'Just the same, I wish you would. I'm not finding fault because you think Keith was murdered, Miss Black. I think he was murdered, too.'

Complete silence fell. A sense of strain that could almost be felt. Mr. Taylor bunched his paper behind him noisily.

'Do you realize what you're saying, Greg?' he demanded. 'There couldn't be a graver charge than murder — and as a legal man I think you ought to know better!'

'I haven't said it was murder without thinking,' Gregory said. 'Just think this over: can you imagine a man committing suicide when he was ready to pay down a deposit on a mortgage on a house for himself and his bride?'

'Greg, what in the world are you talking about?' Pat demanded. 'Keith told me he had ideas about us taking some rooms in Gladstone Avenue — '

'He mentioned that,' Gregory said. 'Two days before he announced his engagement to you he came to see me at the office and said he wanted to find a house, if at all possible, for you and him to live in.'

Pat looked more bewildered than ever. 'Then you knew we were to be engaged before I did!'

'That's true,' Gregory acknowledged, 'but of course I could not say anything: everything was private. Your engagement came as no surprise, naturally. He mentioned that he had an idea about rooms in Gladstone Avenue, but he didn't like the idea one little bit. He said he had some money saved up, and what could I do for him. We do estate agency business, and as it happened there was a house on the books. I didn't see — nor did the boss — why we couldn't fix it for him. He was going to settle the whole thing the day before you got married and give you the deeds as a wedding present . . . So, do you mean to tell me that a man who had planned that far ahead would abruptly decide to commit suicide? My contention is that it is illogical.'

'I don't know so much about that,' Mr. Taylor said, thinking. 'It was proved that he was mentally queer, don't forget. Did you see the colour of his money?'

'No — but I felt sure I would do.'

'I do not seem to remember you saying anything about this at the inquest, Greg,' Pat said tautly. 'You should have done: it might have changed the whole verdict.'

Gregory's pale grey eyes turned on her. 'I don't think it would have made the slightest difference,' he said. 'The jury would have thought as Dad thinks — that it was another crazy notion on the part of Keith. Maybe it was: but I thought it was genuine.'

'And your employer had no comment to make, either,' Maria remarked.

'He didn't know Keith was the person who asked about the house. I merely said a client. As far as I am concerned the matter died when Keith died . . . Now you know why I think he may have been murdered,' Gregory finished grimly. 'And I'm sure you think so, too, Miss Black . . . Which brings me back to my first question.'

'Yes,' Maria acknowledged, 'I believe he was . . . ' And she released a barrage of questions from Mr. Taylor and his wife. She answered the questions composedly, giving as her reasons the same ones she had given Pat.

'But this is appalling!' Mr. Taylor declared, jumping up from the chesterfield and spreading his hands. 'Murder! Here! In this house! Who'd want to do it, anyway?'

Pat seemed to have thrown all reservations overboard.

'Just one person!' she said spitefully. 'That psalm-singing old hypocrite, Mr. Robinson! He hates me — and he hated Keith, too, because he was going to marry me.'

'Ambrose?' exclaimed Mrs. Taylor. 'Ridiculous!'

'Besides,' Mr. Taylor pointed out, 'he couldn't have done anything when he was with us in this very room here. That just doesn't start to make sense . . . '

'Up to now,' Maria said, deciding to quench Pat in case she blurted out too many details in her excitement, 'we have nothing better than a theory to grapple with. I don't mind admitting now that I looked around this afternoon — in the cellar — and failed' to find anything

129

which might suggest how Keith's suicide was . . . arranged.'

'That's no surprise,' Gregory commented. 'I looked in the cellar for myself during last night, when everybody was asleep, and failed to discover anything interesting.'

'Good lord, I wonder if — ' Pat tottered on the very verge of mentioning the candlegrease and stopped herself in time.

'If what?' Gregory asked shortly.

'It's nothing,' Pat muttered, and looked guilty.

Maria gave her a look and remained silent. The same idea, about the candle-fat, had crossed her mind, too. In looking round for himself Gregory might have used a candle with which to look up the chimney — which would account for the grease spots. In that case the foundation would drop out of a theory she had built up . . . She approached the topic warily.

'You looked everywhere, Mr. Taylor?' she asked Gregory. 'I would remark that the light does not penetrate to every corner.'

He looked surprised. 'I know that. I used my torch. I've one handy in my bedroom to see my watch in the night . . . Oh, I didn't miss anything, if that's what you think.'

'Ah . . . ' Maria nodded, and sat back, giving Pat a quick glance.

'Why, if two of you — pretty experienced in criminology — think Keith was murdered, don't we tell the police?' Mr. Taylor asked. 'We might get in a fearful mess for trying to keep things to ourselves.'

'Simply because we can't suggest a thing like murder without very strong proof,' Gregory said. 'The theory I have — like Miss Black's — is not strong enough. It's all based on supposition.'

'All this sounds dreadfully confusing to me,' Mrs. Taylor said. 'If there are no signs of anything, what do you propose to do? How can you go to work on — well, nothing?'

'Obviously we can't,' Maria responded, shrugging. 'So I shall look further — maybe have a chat with Mr. Robinson, too, amongst other things. As long as I remain convinced that murder was done somehow, by someone, I shall never rest.'

'We owe that much to Keith, anyway!' Pat exclaimed, 'If he was murdered — yes, even if his own father was at the back of it — the truth's got to be brought out.'

'Yes, you're right.' Her father made the admission quietly. He was still looking rather dazed.

Gregory Taylor straightened his jacket. 'Miss Black, if there is any way in which I can help, don't forget to ask me. I'm not without experience: I've read crime books and magazines for as long as I can remember. Besides that, I am a legal man.'

'I'll remember that,' Maria replied, nodding. 'But please don't anticipate any extraordinary demonstrations on my part. I merely pick up what I can and then let the pieces fall together as a whole . . . '

The sense of tension returned again. Pat stirred uneasily. 'I — I think I'll make some supper,' she said. 'It's getting near bedtime anyway.'

7

Maria retired at 11.15, but did not indulge in her customary reading once she had settled in bed. Instead she took up a black leather-covered book from the side table — which book she had unearthed from her luggage beforehand — and leafed through it until she came to a clean page. Then, her fountain pen unscrewed, she began writing in a neat, scholastic hand, the book propped on her raised knees.

Quite fortuitously I have stumbled into what I think is murder most ingeniously disguised as suicide — in fact so ingeniously that even the police and the coroner have been misled — but in case I may be in the midst of something important I feel I must record my impressions.

The outstanding problem is how Keith Robinson was murdered. Leaving aside the puzzling fact that he evidently went into the cellar and locked himself in, how did his killer also get to him, kill him by hanging him (for apparently this was the cause of death, there being no other signs of injury) and then get out again without moving the key from the inside of the door and without disturbing anybody in the house? How could this happen in broad daylight with the house full of people? True, they were concentrated in one room, but would any murderer take that appalling risk?

The only commonsense theory is that it could not be done — so I submit the following theories for my own consideration . . .

1. Everybody has sworn that they saw Keith's shadow cast on the whitewashed wall — but they did not see the body itself there and then.

I am inclined to question if it was the shadow of a body, or the cut-out image of a body in front of the light bulb. It need not have been a large image. Distance from the wall would give the image a large size upon projection . . . This thought in mind, I questioned Pat. She said that the image, as far as she could remember, had a hazy quality.

It is questionable whether, at such short notice, Pat could possibly remember what the shadow looked like, but on the possibility that her statement might be correct I suggest that there might have been a small image magnified by distance to large size, which automatically would take the sharpness from the edges of the silhouette.

2. Conceding this theory, I am face to face with an equally great problem. If there was a faked image it surely must have come into view when Keith switched on the light? Yet he made no attempt to beat a hurried retreat from the cellar — and surely he would have done at the sight of the apparent shadow of a hanging man? Or, did the sight fascinate him, and he went to explore — to meet his death somehow at the base of the stairs?

The word 'somehow' is worrying me quite a lot. Either way the problem is baffling, and I don't even know if there was a cut-out. I can only surmise . . .

It is perhaps worthy of note that Gregory Taylor, Pat's brother, knows criminal methods inside out — and as far as I can gather he did not approve of his sister's intended marriage. I merely mention it.

Keith's father also did not approve, and he is a locksmith, which may have something to do with the door being locked on the inside.

Apparently the announcement of Keith's possible incipient insanity was a surprise to everybody except Ambrose Robinson — which makes the motive difficult, to assess except in so far as Ambrose Robinson himself is concerned, But since he did not know of the engagement until a week before the murder — and did not enter the Taylor home during that week — how could he have devised anything in time? Mr. and Mrs. Taylor seem to be more easy-going than anything else, though clearly stunned by the proceedings. As for Pat, knowing her as I do from the days when she was at college, I can't see that she could have had anything to do with it. What had she to gain?

Very important! Grease spots in a grate that is never used. How did the spots get there?

Point for further consideration. Could a man have such a weak constitution that one glass of wine — combined with the excitement of his being engaged, and the heat of the evening — knocked him out flat? Ponder this: it may be very important.

The time is 11.45 p.m.

Maria put the book under her pillow and the pen on the table, then she switched off the light. In ten minutes she was asleep.

★　★　★

Maria arrived at breakfast the following morning at eight o'clock, just as the family was settling. They no longer looked bewildered. Apparently they had all grown accustomed to the idea that it was possible murder had been done.

As though there had been a mutual pact to steer clear of the topic of Keith, nobody referred to it — though now and again Gregory looked as if he were going to say something about it, only to switch to a commonplace topic instead. But, inevitably, it came up as Pat said:

'Keith's funeral's on Monday morning. At the Redford cemetery. There's a letter from Mr. Robinson this morning letting us know. He . . . he didn't invite you Miss Black.'

'If that is supposed to shock me, my dear, it does not,' Maria responded. 'Mr. Robinson hardly knows me, so why should he ask me to be a mourner?'

'I just wondered if perhaps Mr. Robinson knows of your reputation as a criminologist and wants to keep away from you as much as possible — because he's guilty, I mean.'

'You certainly have it in for the unfortunate Mr. Robinson, haven't you?' Maria asked, breaking toast.

'I'm only saying what I think!' Pat retorted.

'Miss Black, have you . . . thought any more about the business?' Mrs. Taylor asked.

'Oh, yes — quite a deal. Only it hasn't

amounted to anything. Just theories! If only I could get my hands on something concrete! I think the only way is to approach the problem by having a word with Mr. Robinson himself.'

'Then you do think as I do!' Pat exclaimed in triumph.

Maria went on with her breakfast. 'Don't jump to conclusions, Pat. I merely wish to get an insight on Keith's life and habits. I cannot imagine anybody better suited than his father to give me the information.'

'But why do you have to go to all that trouble?' Pat frowned. 'What about the can — '

'There must,' Maria interrupted, 'have been more in the life of Keith than has so far come to light.'

'Can?' Gregory Taylor repeated, puzzling. 'What were you going to say about a can, sis?'

'Can?' Pat looked bothered. 'Oh, the can! I was going to say, Miss Black, if you want that petrol you mentioned last night we've a can full in the garage Dad can let you have.'

'That would be very handy,' Maria conceded gravely. 'However, it can wait for the time being. I've more fuel than I thought I had.'

'You mean you want to buy my spare petrol?' Mr. Taylor looked vague. 'Why, sure — any time.' He glanced at his watch. 'Well, I must be off.'

He took his leave a few minutes later, and Gregory was not long following him. Maria, her breakfast finished, sat thinking. Then Mrs. Taylor who made an observation.

'You know, Miss Black, Mr. Robinson — Ambrose as we call him — is a very strange man. You'll discover that when you come to talk to him.'

'I had already noticed his peculiarities,' Maria responded. 'I take it that his tendency to hold forth on the Scriptures is nothing new?'

'He's been doing it ever since we first knew him,' Mrs. Taylor responded. 'That's seven years ago ... He's a big friend of ours, and I think that he has a heart in him somewhere despite his odd manner ... It's queer, but in all the time we've known him he never once hinted that his wife died in — in the way she did.'

'A definitely sad end for the poor woman,' Maria said. 'And sad for Mr. Robinson, too, of course. I can understand that he did not reveal the circumstances of his wife's death. One would hardly advertise a misfortune like that to all and sundry.'

'All he ever did say, to Harry and me — and that was in an unguarded moment — was that his wife died in the Sunbeam Home of Rest. Well, naturally, we never thought of a mental institution. We just assumed it was a private nursing home — though I did wonder a little why he was so quick to drop the subject afterwards. Perhaps he got the idea that we might be inquisitive and start to look into it . . . Of course we didn't: we're not that kind. At that time Keith and Pat weren't walking out together, of course.'

Mrs. Taylor got to her feet and sighed. 'Well, have to start washing-up, I suppose.'

'I'll help you,' Pat said, rising, but her mother waved her hand.

'This lot won't take me more than five minutes. Besides, you have Miss Black to chat to.'

Pat moved away from the table and took up a position by the window, gazing outside. In a moment or two Maria came over to her. Neither of them said anything until Mrs. Taylor had disappeared into the kitchen regions.

'I nearly put my foot in it, didn't I?' Pat asked, looking ashamed. 'I mean about that candle fat ... But since everybody in the house knows now what you are doing, where is the point in being secretive?'

'The point,' Maria answered, 'is that if I explained to the family every move I'm making, one or other of them might let something slip. It is very hard sometimes to keep interesting news under your — er — hat. And a word to the wrong person might get eventually to the ears of the murderer.'

Pat glanced at the clock. 'What about Mr. Robinson? Are you going to see him?'

'Later perhaps. At the moment I would much prefer to have another look in the cellar — this time with a powerful torch I have brought with me.'

'Will it matter if Mother knows what we're doing?'

Maria shrugged. 'I don't see how we can help her knowing — but unless she comes down after us she won't know exactly what we're up to. The more confidential we keep our activities the better.'

Pat went out to the kitchen doorway and called above the noise of splashing water and moving crockery:

'We're both going down in the cellar again, Mum, to have a look round.'

Maria did not catch the response. She was leaving the room. She went upstairs for her torch and returned to the hall to find Pat waiting for her outside the ready opened cellar door.

Together they went down the curving wooden staircase. When they had gained the big old-fashioned fireplace, Pat stood to one side and watched Maria's massive shoulders, as she leaned forward into the grate and peered into the chimney flue, flashing the bright beam of her torch into the sooty void.

'Something occurred to me last night, Miss Black,' Pat said. 'I think we might amend our view that nobody could get up and down that chimney. A really slender person of about my build perhaps could, or even somebody of Keith's dimensions. Suppose somebody did, and carrying a candle? That would account for the grease, wouldn't it?'

'Think again, my dear,' Maria responded, her voice muffled by the looming walls of the fireplace. 'This chimney is not wide enough to permit of the passage of a human being — even of a child — since it narrows as it goes up and then takes a sharp right-angled turn round which nobody could get. Besides, think of the soot such an endeavour would bring down. Think also of what neighbours would think if they saw somebody emerging from your chimney. The murder happened in day-light, don't forget . . . No, that isn't the answer.'

She became silent again for a while, stretching her arm to the limit and flashing the torch beam into the black tunnel; then she said, 'The soot has been disturbed for a distance of about twelve feet up — before the flue narrows. And there seems to be a comparatively new nail on the inside of this flue. Yes! There is!'

She withdrew from her exploration and straightened up.

With an effort Pat fought down a smile. Dignified though her manner was, Maria's face was filthy with soot smudges and little specks of hardened carbon had settled in her hair.

'Unfortunately,' she said gravely, 'my — hmm — proportions prevent my standing up inside the chimney. I am most anxious, though, to get at that nail and examine it —'

'Then that's a job for me!' Pat declared. 'I shan't be a minute. I've got some overalls upstairs — or rather Greg has — and I can borrow them. And a rubber bathing-cap will keep my hair okay. Be back in a moment . . .'

She swung away and went hurrying up the wooden staircase. Maria stroked the end of her long nose pensively, and unwittingly added more smudges to those already present.

Whilst she waited for Pat's return she prowled about the cellar, flashing the powerful torch beam into every corner — but no fresh evidence presented itself.

Then at last there was the sound of Pat's speeding feet above as she came down the staircase from the bedroom. With the energetic zest of youth she came tumbling down the wooden stairs in blue overalls, old gloves, and a bathing helmet

'Well? Will I do?'

Maria smiled at the incongruity of her attire. 'Splendidly . . . Here is the torch.'

It was only the work of a moment for Pat, with her slim figure, to slide into the rusty old grate and gradually worm herself upright. When she spoke her words sounded muffled.

'Yes, Miss Black, there is a nail here.'

'I thought so. New, is it not? I thought I caught a light reflection from it.'

'Yes, it's new all right. A six-incher, tilted slightly upwards. It's been driven in between the bricks I think . . . Huh!'

'What do you mean? Huh?' Maria questioned.

'Oh, nothing. Just that there's a hole in the chimney breast.'

'A hole?' Maria repeated sharply. 'What kind of a hole?'

'As near as I can tell it's about a thirty-second of an inch wide ... You won't be able to see it from the cellar side. I can only see it here because everything's so black — so I can see the cellar light shining through the hole.'

'What is the position of the hole in relation to the nail?' Maria asked, thinking.

'It's about three inches below it — that is the hole is.'

'Mmm — thanks, Pat.' Maria frowned to herself. 'Can you get that nail out?'

There were signs of struggle and a treadmill action of Pat's overalled legs.

'No,' she said finally. 'I can't budge it.'

'All right, never mind. It's of no consequence at the moment. Whilst you are there see if there are any traces of candle-grease round the nail or on the wall into which it is driven.'

Long pause.

'I'll say there are!' Pat exclaimed finally. 'Big splashes of grease directly below the nail — but none above. They're all mixed with soot. It looks to me as though quite a lot of candle-grease has been spilled.'

'Splendid! That is all I wanted to know, Pat. You can come down.'

The girl squirmed her way slowly out of the flue and at length slid out of the grate. She handed the torch back to Maria and then batted at herself vigorously.

'Well, what does that prove?'

'I can't answer that straight off,' Maria said dryly. 'Let's take it step by step, shall we? There is candle-grease below the nail and none above — '

'I've a suggestion,' Pat interrupted. 'A candlestick holder might have been hung on the nail by its handle, and because of that it hung at an angle, of course, and fat started dripping down below.'

'You have not, I suppose, any suggestion to offer as to why anybody should hang a candle in the chimney in that fashion?'

Pat looked disappointed. 'Oh, bother! I

never thought of that.'

'Even if your idea was correct, allowing for the circumference of the candlestick base, the fat would be some four or five inches from the nail. Yet there is fat directly below the nail, didn't you say?'

'Yes,' Pat admitted glumly. 'All right; I'd better start guessing again. It would be plain crazy to hang a candle in a chimney.'

Maria began to slowly pace the concrete floor as she meditated. She almost took hold of her watch-chain and remembered her dirty hands just in time.

'Plainly,' she said, 'a candle itself could not be placed on a round, new nail. The only other answer is that some kind of lamp was used, in which the candle was placed — the lamp hanging on the nail. The fat would probably ooze through the ventilation holes in the bottom of the lamp and splash on to the wall.'

Pat reflected and then looked astonished. 'Yes, I suppose that's possible,' she agreed, 'but why should anybody want a candle in the chimney, lamp or otherwise?'

'For the moment that is not relevant,' Maria decided. 'Have you any idea if there is such a lamp in the house? One that would hold a candle?'

'Yes, there is. It's in the garage at the moment, and it belongs . . . to Greg.'

If Maria thought anything at hearing of the lamp's ownership she did not betray it. Instead her eyes rose to the chimney breast.

'I find your discovery of a hole in the wall extremely intriguing,' she commented. 'I think I might do worse than try and find it.'

She drew the backless chair from beside the wall and stood on it, then she examined the whitewashed wall minutely. After a long search she saw the hole about ten inches above her head on a line with the massive beam crossing the ceiling. Motionless, she stood looking at it and pondering. Pat's smudged face was upturned below, framed in the rubber bathing cap.

'I was right, Miss Black, wasn't I?'

'No doubt of it, Pat. But unfortunately I am not tall enough to examine this hole properly. Have you a pair of steps, or something?'

'Nothing easier,' the girl replied, and hurried up the wooden stairs again. In three minutes she was back and set the steps in position in place of the backless chair.

Maria mounted deliberately, pausing on the penultimate step and examining the hole in the wall closely. It had been driven between the bricks, and it had been done at some time after the whitewashing. The whitewash had flaked away with the hole and the mortar underneath was as yet unmarked by age. It was a very tiny hole and, from the floor, quite invisible.

Slowly Maria shifted her gaze and considered the beam across the ceiling. There was no doubt but what the hole was in a direct line with it.

'Definitely unique!' she murmured finally.

Pat held the steps securely as Maria descended somewhat rheumatically to the floor.

'Do you think that we've got something?' the girl asked eagerly, folding the steps up.

'I know we have, my dear,' Maria responded, 'but the problem is — what? A new nail, a new hole in the wall, splashes of candle-grease, and the possibility of a lantern being used, which lantern you say is the property of your brother . . . Well, what are we to make of all that?'

Pat looked uneasy. 'If that lamp does fit into this, and it belongs to Greg, it sort of points in his direction, doesn't it?'

'Once again you are getting ahead of yourself,' Maria commented. 'We must go forward carefully, step by step. I think I will take a look at this lamp in the garage. And remember, say nothing of what we have discovered down here; not even to your mother.'

'All right,' Pat agreed. 'She's gone out to the shops, by the way, so maybe we'd better clean up before she comes back.'

8

Fifteen minutes later, all signs of their chimney activities removed, Pat and Maria were in the garage. Maria stood beside the partially dismantled car and waited whilst the girl rummaged about in roughly made cupboards, greasy-looking toolboxes, and then amidst a pile of junk on the workbench. In the end she straightened up, baffled.

'That's funny!' she exclaimed. 'It's gone! I know it was here not so long ago because I saw it.'

'Can you remember how long ago?' Maria questioned.

'Why, yes — about a month. A friend of mine had a birthday party about then and she'd decorated one of the rooms. I had the idea of borrowing the lamp for a kind of Chinese lantern effect — then I changed my mind. I know it was in here then, under this bench. It's painted pillar-box red and has glass sides that slide out, and a flat base. You could put either an oil lamp or a candle in it.'

'How very annoying!' Maria muttered, compressing her lips. 'And yet, only to be expected . . . If the lamp had some connection with the death of Keith, whoever was responsible would probably get rid of it.'

'Why?' Pat asked. 'Doesn't that make things all the more suspicious? Wouldn't it have been more sensible to put the lamp back here?'

'It would have been, yes — but the criminal mind has a habit of getting rid of everything connected with a crime. Which, I fancy, is why the lamp has disappeared.'

'We could ask Greg,' Pat said, though she looked doubtful.

'We could — but we won't. Good heavens, girl, don't you realize that asking him a thing like that would sound like an accusation? There must be some other way . . . Tell me, how many people knew that the lamp was in here?'

'Practically everybody could have known it was here, depending on whether they happened to notice it or not. All of us in the family knew, of course — and so did Keith and his father, and Betty Andrews and Madge Banning.'

'Indeed? They had been in here at some time then?'

'In the car. It was running then. When we had a party or anything we picked them up in the car, and if it was raining they got out of the car in the garage here and walked through that house door there. Saved them getting wet. As I say, any of them could have noticed the lamp.'

'Which widens the field instead of narrowing it,' Maria sighed. 'Since the lamp is not here, we have to try and decide where it might have gone . . . How big was it?'

'Oh, about . . . ' Pat spread her hands apart. 'Say six inches high and four inches square, near as I can remember.'

'In other words, not very easily concealed. Is there anywhere handy in this district which might be classed as a waste dump, do you know?'

'I'm afraid there isn't. This is a very thickly built residential area. There isn't an unused spot for miles.'

'Whoever used the lamp,' Maria said slowly, fingering her watch-chain, 'had the opportunity to remove it afterwards and dispose of it. That fact must be borne in mind, and I don't think there is any longer any doubt but that it was used . . .'

'Yes, it's all horribly obvious,' Pat admitted, frowning. 'And since the death of Keith nobody except ourselves has been in the house. I — I don't like it a bit, Miss Black. It indicates that one of us — Mother, Father, or Greg, might have done it. Even *I* might have done it.'

'Mmm — I too have been in the house,' Maria commented, 'and there is also the possibility that Mr. Robinson — if for a moment we view him as the culprit — could have returned in the night and removed the lamp. There would be no difficulty when we were all asleep. A skilled locksmith would experience no trouble in forcing an entry by a window . . . The front and back doors have bolts, have they not?'

'Top and bottom.'

'Then a window could have been used. The cellar door was not locked at that time due to its being smashed. Yes, Mr. Robinson — or an outsider — could have got in, removed the lamp, and gone out again.'

'What other outsider could there be except Mr. Robinson?' Pat questioned, surprised.

Maria spread her hands. 'At the moment I haven't the least idea. I can only gain an insight as to that when I have discovered what kind of acquaintances Keith had. There might even have been enemies of which nothing has been mentioned so far . . . ' Maria came back to her starting-point. The fact remains, where did the lamp go? It could have been taken away completely — to Mr. Robinson's home if he did it. It could also have been thrown in the dustbin. Since the culprit did not know that anybody had any idea that the lamp had been used, what was wrong with throwing it away as refuse?'

Turning aside, Maria left the garage by the yard door and went across to the dustbin standing near the kitchen window. She whipped off the dustbin lid and then looked annoyed. The dustbin had only recently been emptied.

'Yes, they empty it every Friday,' Pat said, coming up. 'Yesterday.'

'Most exasperating!' Maria put the lid back on the bin. 'Let me think . . . As I understand it most municipal destructor works have a magnetic device by which loads of rubbish are sifted — the metallic from the clinkers. I don't fancy exploring rubbish dumps as would a mongrel for a stray bone . . . Besides, I have other things to do. Well, that leaves only one thing for it.'

'I must go,' Pat said.

'No. It's no job for a girl like you, my dear. It's a man's work — and since dustmen are involved, a tough man's work . . . Mr. Martin must do it.'

Pat frowned. 'Mr. Martin? You mean that American chap who helps you sometimes?'

'I mean Pulp Martin — or Horace, to give him his correct name.' Maria cleared her throat gently. 'Yes, indeed — the admirable Mr. Martin will enjoy himself to the full, no doubt, exploring the dumps of a destructor works. There is, of course, no guarantee that the lamp was ever thrown in the bin, but since it is a possibility it must be explored.'

From a pocket of her dress Maria took out a small notebook and studied a series of entries.

'Hmmm — his last residing-place was the 'Smoking Faggot' in Arundel, Derbyshire. I have the telephone number, and presumably he is still there. Doing what, I wonder?'

Maria closed the notebook, and looked at Pat. 'I prefer to keep my contacting Mr. Martin a secret at present. Is there a telephone kiosk nearby?'

'Yes, at the corner of the far end of the street, going into town.'

'Excellent,' Maria said, and added: 'I'll just slip into the house for my hat and sunshade. Then I'll be on my way and ring up Mr. Martin to come over — '

'I — er — ' Pat gave a hesitant little smile — 'I don't want to sound anti-social, Miss Black, but do you think he should stay here? I mean, after all, he — '

'He will stay,' Maria said, 'in Redford at the men's hostel. You need have no fear of him — hmm — polluting the family, my dear.'

Pat looked relieved. 'Oh, well then, that's all right . . . Look, are you going to see Mr. Robinson by yourself, or can I come with you?'

'That is entirely up to you. Since you are inevitably involved in this business I might even find it useful to have you beside me when we interview Mr. Robinson.'

'I'll leave a note for Mum,' Pat said. 'And shall I get your hat and sunshade for you?'

Maria beamed. 'Thank you, my dear.'

With a nod Pat hurried into the house and Maria moved with majestic calm down the drive to her Austin Seven. She had settled behind the driving wheel when Pat finally returned with the hat and sunshade. Maria fixed the hat in position, using the driving mirror to see her reflection. Switching on the ignition, she reversed the car into the road. Then Pat said:

'There's the telephone kiosk at the corner. You can see it from here.'

Maria nodded. The kiosk was only about fifty yards distant. The Austin began to throb gently in its direction.

Maria drew up the car with a jerk and squeezed out into the road. Pat watched her moodily through the windscreen as she compressed herself into the telephone box.

Maria consulted her notebook, and rang the railway station first. She ascertained the arrival times of the trains from Derbyshire, and jotted them in her notebook. Then she placed a long distance call through to Arundel.

For several minutes she argued with an operator until at last a gruff voice from the Midlands responded.

'The 'Smokin' Faggot'! 'Oos that?'

'I understand,' Maria said distinctly, 'that you have a Mr. Martin staying with you. I would like to speak to him. It's most urgent.'

'*Stayin*' with me!' echoed the voice.

'Huh, I like that! 'E's workin' as a barman — hang on and I'll get 'im.'

Maria waited, considering Pat's pale, serious face in the car outside — then a blast from the receiver nearly hurled Maria into the street.

'Yeah, who wants who? An' make it quick!'

'What, Mr. Martin, is the urgency?' Maria asked calmly. 'I am paying for this call, not you.'

'Well, tear out me gizzard and call me chickenhearted! If it ain't Maria! I'd know those pipes any place! Say, where've you been hiding since we monkeyed around with that business with the dame in the Langhom post office — '

'A moment, Mr. Martin, please! Time is precious! I want you to drop whatever you're doing, pack your things, and catch the first train you can to Redford, in Essex.' She consulted her notebook. 'Your train will arrive at the station here at 3.45. I'll be waiting at the station to meet you. You *can* leave more or less immediately, I take it?'

'Sure I can. But what's the angle?'

'I'll tell you personally. I don't trust telephones.'

'Okay. Usual terms, Maria?'

'Of course.'

'Swell!' Pulp Martin enthused. 'I've been waiting for a chance like this to give the guy who runs this clip joint the brush-off. I — '

The warning note sounded and Maria said a hasty goodbye. Smiling to herself, she returned to the Austin Seven and settled once more at the wheel.

'Well, did you get him?' Pat inquired.

'Yes indeed. I've arranged to meet him at the station at 3.45. That leaves us with comfortable time to see Mr. Robinson . . . Direct me, will you? You know where he lives.'

Pat nodded and Maria restarted the engine. When she had given the necessary directions, Pat fell silent for a while, thinking; then she said:

'I've heard about Mr. Martin through the papers, Miss Black, but all they ever said was that he's an American from the Bowery who helps you now and again in criminology. The Bowery bit doesn't sound too salubrious. That was why I was scared of the possibility of him staying with us.'

Maria chuckled. 'If Mr. Martin were not so substantial I should call him the skeleton in my cupboard. I first met him in New York. Later, after making America too hot for himself, he came to England — since when he has remained in this country. How he lives is a complete mystery to me, but it seems to consist of doing anything and everything and staying on this side of the law. He's loud, overpowering — the kind of Bowery thug you have pictured to yourself — and yet he has a heart in him. His fists are powerful, his methods shatteringly to the point. There could be no more useful man for dirty work. I suppose the oddest thing of all is the affinity between us.'

'You're an extraordinary woman, Miss Black,' Pat murmured, smiling. 'For a headmistress, I mean. Nobody would ever expect a headmistress to do the things you do.'

'The headmistress doesn't,' Maria responded dryly. 'It is the criminologist. Call it schizophrenia, call it what you like — but there it is . . . Ah! The estimable Mr. Robinson's, I believe!'

She drew the car to a halt outside a shop in which the blinds were drawn, whilst an oblong card behind the door glass said — *Closed Owing to Bereavement*. Pat joined Maria when she, too, had alighted, and they turned to the house door, Pat pressing the bell vigorously. After a while the tall, sombre Ambrose Robinson snapped back a bolt and appeared in the doorway.

'Oh, Miss Black! Pat!' He looked surprised.

'I'd like a little chat with you, Mr. Robinson,' Maria said.

'Why should you want to chat with me?' he asked, studying Maria intently. 'My boy not yet in the earth and you have to come bothering! What is it?' he demanded petulantly.

'It's very important,' Pat put in, feeling that she ought to be helpful.

'Important?' Ambrose Robinson gave a sigh and gestured behind him. 'Oh, all right. Come inside . . . '

They passed down the narrow hall that separated the shop from the living premises, and entered the small room with which Pat was already familiar.

The remains of a meal were still on the table. Also upon the table was a Bible, open at Joshua. Maria eyed it briefly and then settled on the chair Ambrose Robinson drew forth for her. Pat chose a chair by the fireplace and sat with her toes turned in.

'Now?' Ambrose Robinson asked, standing in front of the empty grate with his hands clasped behind him. 'What is all this about?'

Maria looked up at him. The resemblance to a bird of prey was remarkable, she decided — the sunken cheeks, the hooked nose and pointed chin.

'I think you should know, Mr. Robinson,' Maria said, 'that your son might have been the victim of foul play — and not a suicide.'

'That's impossible.' His expression did not change. 'We all heard the evidence at the inquest; we know that it was death whilst of unsound mind. The simple truth is that Keith had too much of his mother in him — and so he suddenly decided to take his own life. It's all perfectly obvious to me, and if you don't mind I'd much rather not discuss it.'

'There are such things,' Maria said, 'as perfect crimes.'

A frown gathered slowly on Ambrose Robinson's high forehead. 'By what authority do you dare say such things?'

'If you read newspapers as thoroughly as you do your Bible, Mr. Robinson, you'd know!' Pat said, rather hotly.

Ambrose Robinson looked at her. 'I suppose,' he said coldly, 'you don't mean to be impertinent?'

'I'm simply stating a fact.' Pat got up from her chair and began moving about, the better to emphasize her words. 'Truth is, Miss Black is a criminologist. Professionally she is a headmistress — but she's also an expert on crime. That fact has been reported in the newspapers many a time — as you'd know if you ever read any.'

Ambrose Robinson looked astonished. 'You mean, madam, you are a private detective?'

Maria spread her hands. 'To quote the immortal Sherlock, Mr. Robinson, I am 'interested in crime — and criminals'.'

'Then I strongly disapprove!' Ambrose Robinson snapped. 'By what right do you dare meddle in so serious a business? What possible proof can you have?'

'I have all the proof I consider necessary,' Maria answered quietly. 'Naturally, you wonder why I don't inform the police? Simply because I do not think they would listen to me — '

'I should think they would not! So why tell me?'

'I would not even have told *you* that it is possible your son had met with foul play, but for the fact that Gregory Taylor thinks so, too . . . ' Only the icy glint in Maria's eyes showed how much Ambrose Robinson had stroked her fur the wrong way. 'Since he does think so there is no reason why he might not say so to you — and add that I agree with him. I dislike a story second-hand, and you may do so as well. That is why I am here to state my beliefs.'

'All my family think he was murdered!'

Pat declared. 'Miss Black has given me certain proofs which show Keith could not have done the thing he did in committing suicide.'

'What are you talking about?' Ambrose Robinson demanded.

'I do not believe,' Maria said, 'that Keith had sufficient time to choose the 'site' for his suicide upon so short an acquaintance with the cellar . . . ' Then as she saw that Robinson was still unconvinced she launched into greater detail, giving the story much as she had given it to Pat. But she did not mention a word about her discoveries in connection with the candle grease, the hole in the chimney, and the lamp.

'Slender evidence,' Ambrose Robinson muttered at length, 'and yet logical enough, since it is based on considered opinion.' He sat down at the uncleared table. Resting his elbows on it, he considered Maria thoughtfully. ' "The tongue of the just is as choice silver",' he muttered. ' "The heart of the wicked is of little worth . . . ' Proverbs.'

Pat gave a disgusted look and went

back to her chair. Maria sat back and fondled her watch-chain gently.

'Naturally,' she said calmly, 'I do not claim to be infallible, though as a general rule I must say that I have achieved results from my theories. Because I believe your son was the victim of a cleverly executed crime, I am trying to gather whatever information I can about him, in the hope that I may finally tear the whole plot against him to pieces.'

'Why?' Ambrose Robinson asked, puzzled. 'You didn't even know Keith.'

'I am a lover of justice, Mr. Robinson, and I enjoy a puzzle in crime above all things . . . Surely you wish the real facts concerning your son's demise to be unearthed?'

'By all means, but — well, I just don't know what to think. The police and the coroner seem to be certain that it was suicide.'

'That, I fancy, is exactly what Keith's murderer wanted them to think . . . ' Maria reflected for a moment, then: 'What I particularly wish to know is — what happened on the night of the engagement? I understand Keith was intoxicated?'

'I'll go further than that,' Ambrose Robinson said. 'He was dead drunk.'

'On one glass of wine?' Maria sounded sceptical.

'He *said* it was only one glass. More likely it was half a dozen.'

'It was not, and you know it!' Pat declared flatly. 'We all testified to that at the trial. One glass and no more. How far do you think a bottle of wine stretches?'

'All right, Pat, if you say so,' Ambrose Robinson sighed. 'But in my opinion there was no need even for that! Keith never took an intoxicating drink in his life until that night. He wouldn't have done so then, either, except for being urged into it.'

'How do you know he never had one in his life?' Maria asked pensively.

'Since I do not smoke my sense of smell is exceptionally keen. Had he ever drunk any intoxicant I should have known about it — as I did on that night. I detected it about Pat, too.'

'Oh, this is crazy!' Pat said impatiently.

171

'I had the same amount as Keith. I don't pretend I never had an intoxicant before — but all it did was make me feel comfy inside. And I'm a girl!' she pointed out. 'Supposed to be weaker than a man. Keith had the same as me and passed out . . . I still don't understand it.'

'Neither do I,' Maria said, thinking. 'What happened *exactly*? Was he intoxicated when you walked home with him, Pat?'

'No; he didn't seem to be. His walk was steady and his conversation wasn't slurred or anything.'

'It came on him suddenly, as Pat will verify,' Ambrose Robinson said, brooding. 'He collapsed without the least warning and remained in a drunken stupor until eleven o'clock. That was about three hours of insensibility.'

'And did he have a — hmm — hangover?'

'He said he did.'

'It seems an incredible thought,' Pat said musingly, staring at the rug, 'but do you suppose his wine was perhaps drugged?'

'That thought is by no means incredible,' Maria remarked. 'In fact it is the only logical assumption.'

'But that's absurd!' Ambrose Robinson protested. 'Where would be the sense of it? Pat, or her brother — or father or mother — would never do such a thing.'

Maria shifted her gaze to the girl. 'Pat, when you walked here with Keith you didn't meet anybody, did you? Perhaps collide with somebody?'

'No. Far as I can remember we didn't pass a soul.'

'And about how long was it, after you had arrived here, when Keith collapsed?'

'I'd say about ten minutes,' Pat answered, and Ambrose Robinson nodded confirmation.

'Ten minutes . . . Hmmm. And he didn't have anything to eat or drink whilst he was here?'

Both heads shook in firm negation.

'If he was drugged,' Ambrose Robinson said deliberately, 'only somebody in the Taylor family could have done it. That's perfectly plain.'

'Yes, but — ' Pat looked uneasy. 'Look

here, what on earth could have been the idea behind it? It didn't lead to anything. It only made Keith fall dead asleep for a time. Unless . . . ' Pat stopped, and from her expression she did not appear to like the thought that had occurred to her.

'Unless what?' snapped the locksmith, a glint in his bulgy eyes.

'Nothing,' Pat said, shaking her head. She was resolved in her own mind that she would only relate what had occurred to her when she was alone with Maria.

Maria said: 'The possibility of Keith's having been drugged is a point I must consider very carefully. I agree that it seems he could have received the drug only at the hands of one of the Taylors — unless he administered it himself. I have got to be quite sure of this angle, otherwise we're getting into a region of dangerous accusation, and that won't do . . . Tell me, Mr. Robinson, had your son any enemies?'

'Enemies? Not as far as I'm aware. Actually, I think that he regarded me as his worst enemy. I tried to show him the evils of this world, as mentioned at the trial, but he wouldn't listen to me. He believed I was only trying to block his progress. My only wish was to keep him as separate from the world as possible because I knew, long ago, that he had inherited the same terrible affliction as his mother. When I knew he was going to be married I was faced with a problem. I let him think I did not want to lose him, but I only incurred his enmity through doing that. My main wish was to try and make him break off the engagement, without telling him why . . . I was unsuccessful.'

'And his death solved your problem?' Maria asked quietly.

'Yes. In that sense I was grateful for it.' Ambrose Robinson looked at her sharply. 'But if you are thinking that I — '

'I am not thinking anything of the kind, Mr. Robinson: I am merely making a statement . . . If his death had not intervened I take it you were intending to let him go through with the marriage, knowing what you did about him?'

'No. At the risk of what might happen I was fully prepared to stop the ceremony by saying I knew just cause and impediment. It might not have stopped the marriage, of course, but at least my own conscience would have been clear . . . '

'Wouldn't it have been a little more honest to have told *me* and let me make my own decision?' Pat asked bitterly.

'Yes,' Ambrose Robinson admitted, sighing. 'Perhaps it would — but as I tell you, my main wish was to try and make Keith call off the marriage without knowing the real reason for doing so. That, I'm afraid, is why I tried to poison his mind against you, Pat, why I laid such emphasis on the curse of drink.'

'Oh!' Pat's dark eyes were coldly resentful. 'So that was it!'

'Instead, Keith died . . . hating me,' Ambrose Robinson mused for a moment, then he murmured, ''Sorrow is better than laughter for by the sadness of countenance the heart is made better'. Ecclesiastes.'

Maria rose to her feet and Ambrose Robinson got up, too.

'What do you intend to do, Miss Black?' he questioned. 'Do you intend to pursue this — er — astounding notion that my son was murdered?'

'To the end, Mr. Robinson.'

'I don't like it,' he said curtly. 'My boy died, and the law has said it was suicide. Why can't you let it rest at that?'

'You would surely not prefer that your son should, be remembered as a suicide?' Maria asked. 'It is hardly a pleasant reflection to have cast upon him when it is not true.'

'I would much rather leave the whole thing alone. It is too harrowing a business — '

'Harrowing or otherwise, the truth has to be found,' Maria said, in her most didactic voice. 'I mean to continue my investigation. Somebody meant to make sure that your son never married Pat — and, so far, I have been of opinion that the motive was to prevent his — er — mental trouble being transmitted to possible children . . . There is, however, the possibility that he was murdered for some other reason entirely.'

'What other reason?' Ambrose Robinson asked grimly.

Maria shrugged. 'Perhaps somebody

didn't like the idea of his having Pat — somebody who wanted Pat for himself. In other words a crime of jealousy. It is a possibility we cannot ignore.'

'Miss Black, you can't mean Billy Cranston or Cliff Evans?' Pat exclaimed, her eyes widening. 'They'd never do a thing like that! Besides, they didn't have the slightest opportunity. I haven't seen either of them for long enough.'

'Anybody would do anything, my dear, if they considered it was justified,' Maria stated. 'That was why I asked you, Mr. Robinson, if your son had any enemies. Apparently he had not, so far as *you* know. That still does not do away with the possibility of jealous enemies who didn't want him to have Pat.'

'I think,' Ambrose Robinson said, after some deliberation, 'that all these facts should be placed before the police.'

'As you wish — but be mindful of the fact that you will have to bear out your assertions with proof before the police will act. Even I cannot provide proof — only theories. If you can do better, then do.'

A hopeless look went over the locksmith's gaunt features. 'No, I can't,' he confessed, sighing. 'Very well, Miss Black, do what you think is best in the circumstances. I shan't try and stop you. In fact I'll help you wherever I can. I see now the wisdom of your ideas: if Keith was murdered then the slayer must be found. If in the end you find that you have been wrong, no harm will have been done,'

'I am not wrong,' Maria answered quietly. 'Be assured of that. And thank you, Mr. Robinson, for all that you have told me . . . '

9

As Maria drove back towards the Taylor home, Pat had a good deal to say.

'If anybody had a really good motive for wanting to be rid of Keith that psalm-singing old buzzard had! I've never liked him, Miss Black, even though I've known him for such a long time. I don't ... *trust* him. I don't believe that any man who spouts Scripture to the extent he does can be genuine.'

Maria smiled faintly, her attention on her driving

'My dear girl, because Mr. Robinson 'spouts' Scripture as you poetically put it, it does not necessarily cast his character in doubt. He probably finds that sayings from the Scriptures express his emotions far better than everyday language. Some people have a penchant for reciting quotations to get their point over more clearly. Certainly I don't think there is any significance in the point ... I do, however, think that Mr. Robinson has some difficulty in keeping his mind fixed on one thing at a time. He repeated himself several times and, in places, even went back on himself. Most unusual. Maybe his nerves are not overstrong.'

'Maybe lots of things,' Pat said, folding her arms and sitting back stubbornly in the bucket seat. 'And I still don't like him! Oh, that reminds me! A thought occurred to me whilst you were talking to him about that drug . . . '

'A thought? About what?'

'About Greg, and the way he took the announcement of my engagement. He showed, without actual words, that he thoroughly disapproved of the idea. Had he wanted I'm sure he could have drugged Keith's wine when the attention of the rest of us was diverted. But if he did, I can't for the life of me think what his object could be.'

'At this stage,' Maria said, 'I think we should leave the possibility of drugged wine in abeyance — at least until we have some more definite proof. There are so many other angles to consider . . . '

They returned home to find that Mrs. Taylor had got back from her shopping: she was making preparations for lunch. To her natural curiosity Maria only gave matter-of-fact answers, which did not give away any details. She adopted similar tactics when Mr. Taylor and Gregory — home at lunchtime for the weekend — also plied her with questions. They had to accept her reserve, but the look in the eyes of Gregory, at least, showed he did not like it.

It had reached three o'clock before Maria announced that she had to drive to the railway station, in order to meet a friend. She excused herself and went out into the hall, en route for her bedroom. Pat followed and stopped her as she was about to ascend the stairs.

'Miss Black, are you going to meet Mr. Martin?'

'Yes, indeed.'

'I'd rather like to meet him,' Pat said.

'Before this business is over you probably will do — and should that happen I would warn you to look out for yourself. Mr. Martin has a most disturbing proclivity for chasing — er — shapely young ladies.'

Pat chuckled. 'That makes him more interesting than ever!'

Pat's inner hope that she might go to the station with Maria in the Austin were dashed. Maria decided on going by herself. She had much to discuss with Pulp when he put in an appearance — which he did at exactly 3.45.

The train had hardly been in the station three minutes before Maria, watching intently from the driving seat of her car, saw Pulp emerge with his swinging, vigorous stride from the station exit.

She sounded the car horn twice. Pulp turned, saw the car, and waved an arm vigorously.

Horace — 'Pulp' — Martin was a big man, easily six feet tall and proportionately broad. His attire still betrayed a profound lack of taste. He was wearing a greenish-coloured suit, with tan shoes and a red tie. The June blaze had made him forsake his pork-pie hat and instead his upstanding thatch of red hair seemed more wiry than ever.

'If it ain't Maria!' he declared loudly, stopping by the car's open window and dropping his suitcase to the pavement. 'Shake, Maria! How's tricks?'

His vast red hand shot in at her and swallowed up her palm. She smiled dignifiedly at the vision of his red face, stopped-short nose, and blue eyes. It was an impudent and yet a genial face. As for the eyes, they had that kind of blueness that cannot recognize danger even when looking straight at it.

'So glad to see you again, Mr. Martin,' Maria responded. 'Come along in — round the other side.'

'You betcha!' He swept up his suitcase. 'Same old jollopy, huh? Nice going . . . '

In another moment he had yanked open the opposite door with a force that made the small car rock, wangled his suitcase to the floor behind the front seats, and then he slid into position and grinned amiably.

'I've been waitin' for something like this to happen for long enough, Maria,' he declared. 'Seems to be the heck of a while since I saw you.'

'It will be a year in September,' Maria responded. 'Apparently you have managed to keep body and soul together in the meantime. You look disgustingly healthy.'

'I get by,' he said, shrugging. 'But believe you me, that barman's job at the 'Smokin' Faggot' was the pay off. I only took it so's I could ditch a coupla guys who was on the prod for me. I got 'em out on a limb, see, and I guess they didn't like it.'

Maria knitted her brows. 'Which, analysed, means that you indulged in a gentle swindle and they sought revenge?'

'You got it,' Pulp agreed, nodding. 'Anyway, what's the set-up here? You're ways off your course from your college for hip-swingers, ain't you?'

Maria coughed primly. 'To get down to cases, I am investigating a murder cunningly contrived to look like suicide — and between ourselves it has many aspects which are decidedly puzzling.'

'A humdinger, huh?' Pulp folded his massive, green-suited arms. 'Okay, what's the layout? Mebby I'll have an angle or two. This sort of weather gives me bubbles in me think-tank.'

In all the time she had known Pulp Martin, Maria had never withheld facts from him. She knew that as far as his relationship to her was concerned, he was integrity itself. He never repeated anything he had been told, unless so instructed. Further, there had been times when it had been revealed that his high forehead had its uses. Intelligence and pugilism were weirdly mixed in this forthright product of the Bowery.

In fifteen minutes he had all the facts to date.

'Yeah, it's a lulu,' he confessed. 'Somebody pulled a nice job with this necktie party, Maria . . . And if you ask me, this guy Ambrose Robinson comes in for the heck of a large slice of suspicion. He was the only one who knew his son were as nutty as a fruitcake . . . Although didn't you say that this guy Robinson mentioned some place that his old woman had died in the Sunbeam Home of Rest? Well, one of 'em in the Taylor family could have looked up what the place was, and found out that Mrs. Robinson was loco. Couldn't they?'

'Yes, indeed,' Maria assented. 'I had thought of that.'

'You had, huh? Mighta known it. On the other hand there's this chap Gregory Taylor.' Pulp mused with his eyes narrowed. 'He might have heard something some place about this Sunbeam Home. If so, he might have had a lot to do with the crime. Seems to me as though that lamp, and him readin' detective magazines, makes for a sort of tie-up some place.'

'Again, Mr. Martin, I agree with you,' Maria said. 'However, let us turn to the matter of the drug. What do you imagine was the purpose of that?'

'I dunno — bust me suspenders if I do.'

Maria sighed. 'I'm convinced it had a reason, though what it was escapes me . . . Later, perhaps, it'll dawn on me.'

'You can trust Pat Taylor and old man Robinson, I suppose?' Pulp asked, thinking. 'I mean they ain't working in cahoots and just sayin' that Keith folded up?'

'I think they are perfectly straight about it,' Maria said. 'And telling independent tales. I cannot see them working in conjunction, for they don't like each other.'

'Suppose this guy Keith drugged himself for some reason?'

'It's possible — but what reason?'

Pulp grinned. 'Search me, Maria! Anyway, I guess you want me to start rootin' for a lamp that's had a candle in it, huh?'

'Exactly — first thing on Monday morning. The weekend intervenes, unfortunately.'

'Yeah.' Pulp looked disappointed. 'Don't reckon much to Sundays, Maria: I don't go for that prayer-smitn' stuff . . . Okay, I'll find that destructor works on Monday mornin', if only from its stink.'

'Hmm — quite so . . . Now there are other things to be considered. You have to domicile yourself, and I would suggest the Young Men's Hostel in the Redford High Street. In driving past I noticed that there are vacancies.'

Pulp frowned. 'Say, wait a minute!

Ain't I comin' to the Taylor home with you? Where this gal Pat is?'

'No, you are not,' Maria replied decisively. 'For one thing there is no room for an extra visitor, and for another I know your tendencies when it comes to attractive young ladies.'

'Okay.' Pulp grinned widely, not in the least disturbed. 'Keep me mind on the job, huh? As you say.'

Maria switched on the ignition. 'I'll drive you as far as the hostel, Mr. Martin, and then I can safely leave things with you. Here is your usual fee . . . ' She handed him money from her bag. 'I suggest we meet again on Monday, at — ' she reflected — 'say three p.m. That should give you time to find the lamp.'

'Okay. At the station again?'

'No. Our meeting-place will be outside the Rialto Cinema — which you can see there in the distance . . . We will then discuss further.'

'It's a deal, Maria. I guess there couldn't be anything squarer than that.'

★　★　★

On her return to the Taylor home Maria maintained her non-committal attitude — even to Pat — going no farther than saying that she had met her friend. Maria had no doubt that Pat would have asked many more questions, only the arrival of her brother from a football match stopped her. Her father came soon afterwards and Pat had to give up the attempt at questioning.

Gregory Taylor, apparently, had been doing some thinking during the afternoon. 'Do you still believe Keith was murdered, Miss Black, or has your theory come unstuck?' he inquired, as they all sat down to a meal.

'He was murdered, Mr. Taylor.' Maria munched contentedly. 'Cleverly — ingeniously. And, since you yourself also think he was murdered, why do you suggest that my theory might have come . . . unstuck?'

'We might both have guessed wrong, that's all . . . What I want to know is, whom do you suspect? It isn't very pleasant to know somebody has been murdered in your house and not have the least idea who did it.'

'True, but that is the position at the moment,' Maria responded. 'And until I do have some evidence there doesn't seem to be much point in prolonging the discussion.'

Gregory, looking extremely unconvinced, went on with his meal. Then looked at Pat.

'How much do you know about this business, Pat? You've been tagging around with Miss Black most of the time, haven't you?'

'Well, yes, I have,' Pat looked uncomfortable, 'but I don't know any more than she does. In any case I'm no detective.'

'Weren't you going to see Ambrose Robinson, Miss Black?' Mr. Taylor asked, looking up. 'What happened?'

'We discussed at some length the singular fact that Keith collapsed after a single glass of wine.'

'Rather odd, that,' Mr. Taylor said, musing. 'He wasn't what one would call a tough young man — but all the same I'm sure he wasn't all that weak.'

'I've been thinking about that,' Greg remarked, putting down his knife and fork. 'If he was tight the effect would, I maintain, have been evident within five minutes of having had the drink. Intoxication isn't a thing that suddenly descends and knocks you flat. So I suggest that he wasn't intoxicated at all — but drugged!'

'Oh, lor'!' Pat muttered, and gave a helpless look at Maria.

Unperturbed, Maria took up the conversation. She knew that it was more than possible that Ambrose Robinson might meet one or other of the family before long and relate exactly what had been discussed.

'Your idea of a drug is precisely my own,' Maria said. 'Pat and I discussed the possibility with Mr. Robinson. To my mind a drug is the only explanation — '

'But what the devil — excuse me,' Mr. Taylor apologized. 'Why a drug? What good would that do?'

'I have been over that question so much my mind refuses to work on it any more,' Maria sighed.

'And in the process I'll wager you've had some pretty suspicious thoughts about us!' Gregory snapped.

'I understand that all of you were present around the wine. Since none of you others seemed to be affected in that fashion, and Keith had no contact with anybody save Pat whilst on the way to his home — and the fact that he didn't either drink or eat when he got there — the only possible answer is that he had the drug administered here! By one of you!'

Tense, hostile silence. Maria went on with her meal for a while, then she lowered her knife and fork and said:

'That knotty little problem can be straightened out if one of you will admit why you did it. If you don't . . . Well, it will be found out sooner or later.'

Gregory's thin lips tightened. 'It looks to me,' he said deliberately, 'as though you are calling one of us at this table a murderer!'

'For a legal man, Mr. Taylor, you exaggerate,' Maria commented. 'The *murder* is not even under discussion — only the strange problem of Keith's collapse from a possible drug.'

The silence deepened in the hot room.

Mrs. Taylor darted an anxious glance round the faces as though half afraid of what was going to happen next. At length Gregory spoke moodily.

'*I* drugged Keith's wine,' he said.

His father dropped his knife and fork with an unnerving clatter to his plate.

'In heaven's name, why?' he demanded.

Gregory gave him an odd look, then he said: 'It was sleeping draught. Soluble pills. I didn't like the idea of sis marrying him and my hope was that the drug would work faster than it did and make him seem to be intoxicated. Instead he must have held up until he got home, then the effect struck him down all at once ... Funny thing with a drug. It works so differently on different people.'

'But, for heaven's sake,' Pat cried, 'you surely didn't think I'd not marry Keith just because he'd collapsed from one little drink?'

'I thought,' Greg said haltingly, 'that it would seem to you that he was an utter weakling. You're a strong, healthy sort of girl, the last one in the world to marry a weak man. I felt sure it would make you think twice about marrying him.'

'Then you haven't much insight as to my character,' Pat replied sourly. 'If anything it only made me feel sorry for him — more determined than ever to marry him. Of all the low-down, mean tricks!'

Gregory remained silent and kept his eyes on his plate. His father was still staring at him as if he could not believe what had been said.

'But why *shouldn't* Pat have married him?' Mrs. Taylor demanded, puzzled. 'What had you against him, Greg? You didn't know at that time that he was . . . well, as he was. Did you?'

'No, I didn't know that,' Greg admitted. 'I just had a profound dislike for the chap, that's all, and I didn't want sis to chain herself up to him if by simple methods I could make her change her mind.'

'Everything else apart, it was a despicable thing to do!' Pat flared. 'And if you'd descend to that sort of thing, why shouldn't you also plan his murder?'

'Take it easy, Pat,' her father said sharply.

Gregory shrugged. 'We're discussing the drug, sis. Suppose we keep things in hand?'

'You — you had the sleeping-pills with you, then?' Mrs. Taylor asked, emerging from thought. 'I mean, you must have had because you didn't leave the room to get them. You were present all the time from the engagement being announced to the wine being drunk.'

'I seem to remember,' Pat said, 'that Keith told Greg some days *before* about the engagement, when he asked about that house. That gave you time to prepare, didn't it, Greg?'

'It did — but I didn't,' he replied. 'How was I to know wine would be drunk in celebration? As a matter of fact the idea came to me suddenly. I'd bought sleeping pills that very day. Not been sleeping too well this hot weather, and plenty of hard work on my mind at the office. I'd been wondering what to do to make you dissatisfied with Keith — so I risked doping his wine when nobody was on the watch.'

'The pills were in your pocket then?'

Maria questioned.

'That's right.' Gregory looked at her. 'That's all there was in it — honestly.'

Maria gave what sounded like a satisfied little sigh.

'Well, at least that is the immediate problem of the drug solved . . . Thank you for being so frank.'

Gregory did not add any more. His expression even suggested that he considered he had said too much already. In an aura of definite tension the meal proceeded and so came to an end. Mrs. Taylor rose and began clearing away the crockery, Pat helping her, her face still grim at the revelations of her brother.

Mr. Taylor, his geniality considerably sobered, retired to the chesterfield to tackle the evening paper. Gregory got up and went to an armchair in the corner, beside which on the floor was a stack of magazines. Maria's eyes, as she sat in a basket-chair and mused, followed his movements. She hardly saw him after a while: her thoughts had begun to wander round the problem.

Greg's statement did not, to Maria's

way of thinking, carry a shred of conviction. That a man of Gregory's legal turn of mind should administer a drug on the spur of the moment, in the hope that it would produce similar effects to intoxication and thereby turn his sister away from the idea of marriage, was definitely wrong somewhere. Part of the explanation had been revealed certainly, but by no means all of it.

A sudden remark from Gregory interrupted her thoughts.

'Who in blazes has been messing about with my magazines?' he demanded — and his question appeared to be directed at Pat, who had just come in from the kitchen.

'What magazines?' she asked shortly.

Gregory pointed to the dozen or so crime magazines scattered around his chair. 'These,' he complained. 'They're all mixed up, for one thing, and the cover has been torn off one of them. Look at it!'

He whipped up the magazine in question and waved it in the air. The front cover had definitely gone and the contents page was exposed. Maria studied the magazine as it waved about in Greg's hand. It was a copy of *Super Crime Stories*, though at her distance she could not see the date. Without doubt the magazine was American. The back cover, still intact, was asking in glaring letters if anybody wanted muscles like those of the advertiser.

'I don't know anything about your confounded magazines,' Pat retorted, 'beyond the fact that they clutter the place up when we try to clean.'

Gregory fumed silently and tossed the magazine down. Then his annoyance spilled over again.

'Here am I, all set to read through a serial I've collected for the past few months, and I find all the magazines out of sequence! It's not good enough! Besides, I mean to sell these one day — or exchange 'em. The one with the missing cover makes the sequence useless.'

'As if there weren't more important things,' Pat said irritably. 'Frankly, Greg, it beats me how you can spend your time reading a crime serial when there's crime in our own house.'

Gregory did not respond. He was sorting out his magazines, a look of profound disgust creasing his features. Maria's eyes followed Pat as she finally settled on a hassock near the empty fireplace.

After a while Maria did not see Pat; she did not see anything. She was juggling with the interesting thought that the cover page of a magazine was missing.

Maria retired early with the excuse that she had had an exhausting day. The statement no doubt sounded convincing, to all but Pat. She had too many college memories of Maria's vast energy to believe it, and inwardly she wondered if anything was brewing. As a matter of fact there was. Maria had retired early because she had made up her mind to be abroad during the night, solely for the purpose of looking through the magazines which Gregory Taylor had collected. In other words she was intending to play what she understood was a 'hunch'.

In her room, Maria settled in bed

whilst it was still twilight. Her bedwrap about her shoulders, and her black book resting at an angle on her upraised knee, she wrote steadily:

1. I am more inclined than ever to question if it was a genuine hanging body that the party saw from the head of the cellar steps.

2. It is now definitely revealed that Gregory Taylor drugged Keith's wine — but I do not for one moment credit his explanation as to why he drugged it. He is far too keen a man to administer a drug in the hope that it would produce an apparent intoxication — for which reason (it being suggested that Keith was such a weakling he could not stand one drink) his sister would think twice about marrying. Most unconvincing. There must have been another reason. Allow this to jell.

3. I cannot advance much further until I have traced the whereabouts of a lamp that I am sure was used in the enactment of the crime. I have the estimable Mr. Martin dealing with this matter.

4. The matter of a torn cover from a crime magazine interests me a lot, but I shall draw no conclusion from this until I have verified the suspicion at the back of my mind.

I feel that I am entitled, on the psychological side, to draw certain conclusions at this point. There is no doubt, as Reik has so brilliantly stated in his *Unknown Murderer*, that murderers rarely leave their deeds alone. Some try to incriminate somebody else; others follow every detail of the investigation; still others write insulting letters to the investigators. At root, this is self-betrayal, that irresistible force which the guilty cannot overcome. As a case in point I do well to remember Kurten, the mass-murderer, who followed the police so closely he gave himself away. So, in this matter of murder-psychosis, whom have we in the present set-up? We have Patricia, who is very earnestly following every detail of my investigation; we have her brother, who seems able to anticipate most of my moves. Is it because he is legally agile and so able to forecast (backed by knowledge from crime stories), or is it because he knows what has happened?

On the other hand, the real criminal may have read somewhere of this fatal tendency to self-betrayal, and so has assumed a negative, uninterested attitude which makes my task infinitely more difficult . . .

As ever in a murder problem, there are the two aspects to consider. One thing I do notice, however: there does not seem to be any attempt to incriminate anybody else. The murderer obviously believed the suicide to be so perfect a crime as to render deflection of guilt unnecessary . . .

The time is 9.58 p.m.

Maria nodded to herself, put the book under the pillow, her fountain pen on the bedside table, and then composed herself for slumber. Her cast-iron constitution made her capable of forgetting every-thing and relapsing into dreamless slumber at any time, anywhere. She was half dozing when she suddenly opened her eyes wide under the impact of an idea upon her subconscious.

'That's *it*!' she breathed. 'The drug was an *experiment*! A test! To see how long it took to operate on a man of Keith's constitution . . . Remarkable!' She wagged her head to herself. 'These borderline impressions between the waking and sleeping states are definitely of priceless value . . . '

The problem of the drug having been advanced a stage further, Maria slept on it, until by self-training she awakened herself at exactly three in the morning. Snapping on the bedside light, she looked at her watch and smiled to herself.

'Precision and perfection,' she murmured. 'Excellent!'

She scrambled out of bed and into her dressing gown and slippers. Then taking the fountain pen torch from the dressing table she glided to the door and opened it. There were no sounds, and presumably the entire Taylor family had retired. A loose board on the landing gave Maria a troublesome moment, then she went on downstairs and into the drawing room, heading directly towards the pile of magazines beside the armchair in the corner by the fireplace.

Kneeling down, she began to sort through them until she came to the one without a cover. She inspected the magazine carefully and found that the serial Gregory had referred to was, in this issue, in its fourth instalment.

'In which case,' Maria muttered, 'it would not have the cover painting. The cover, I imagine, would be given to the lead novelette. Hmmm . . . most intriguing.'

The lead novelette was classed as a fifteen-thousand-worder, with the title of 'Swing It, Baby'.

'Extraordinary,' Maria murmured. 'No doubt referring either to that preposterous jive business or . . . a hanging body. *Double-entendre*, I imagine.'

She began reading the opening paragraphs of 'Swing It, Baby' in the glow of her torch, and then gave a start as the electric light suddenly snapped on. She turned her head sharply. Pat was standing in the doorway, hair flowing, gown over her pyjamas. Her face was pale and puzzled, her eyes watching darkly.

10

Pat's voice was low as she spoke.

'What on earth are you doing, Miss Black?'

Maria beamed as she swiftly got the situation in hand.

'I'm afraid I went to bed too soon, my dear. I have had my sleep and am now at a loss as to how to pass the rest of the night. I remembered these crime magazines — for which I have a passionate liking, as you know — so I came down to borrow one.' She folded the magazine so that Pat could not tell it was the one without a cover. 'This one I consider quite interesting. The lead novelette is 'Swing It, Baby'.'

'Oh? Is it?' Pat looked at the magazine's folded back cover and then at Maria. 'You mean you actually read that sort of junk, Miss Black?'

'Junk? Oh, come now, Pat — some poor hardworking writer has no doubt sweated blood trying to write this. Even if he hasn't I shall still enjoy it . . . Incidentally,' Maria added, 'how did you know I was down here?'

'I wasn't asleep,' Pat answered wearily. 'I seem to have such a lot on my mind. I heard that board creak on the landing so I came to see what was going on.'

'Ah . . . you don't suppose your brother will mind my borrowing this, do you?'

'He probably will: you saw how he went up in the air earlier just because somebody had messed up the sequence for him . . . All I can say is let him put up with it!'

'You are not feeling very kindly towards him after his revelations concerning the drugged wine, are you?'

'No, I am not!' Pat said. 'Would you?'

'Probably not . . . Anyway, this is neither the place nor the time for a discussion. I think I shall return to bed. Good night, Pat.'

' 'Night, Miss Black.'

Pat watched Maria depart and then she turned to the pile of magazines and sorted through them slowly. It did not take her long to discover that the only one missing was the one without a cover. She straightened up again, reflected, then switched off the light and returned upstairs. As she passed Maria's room she saw light gleaming under the door.

Maria, quite engrossed, spent half an hour reading the novelette. Only when she had come to the end of it did she lay the magazine aside.

'Yes indeed, Maria. Could be — as our American friends would say. The pity is that Pat surprised me getting the magazine. She'll be bound to tell her brother about it . . . Or will she? Perhaps not, considering their present attitude towards each other. Hmmm. I might do worse than risk returning this to the pile.'

She made a note of the magazine's title, the month, and the year, and then for the second time glided downstairs taking care this time to stride over the loose board. She was back again in her room in three minutes without having been detected. Next she began to write a rough synopsis of the story in her record book. Though she had ample faith in her memory she also believed in writing down points that might become blurred in the movement of events:

'Swing It, Baby' is the story of a young man who falls in love with a worthless chorine. This 'gold digger', as I think she is called, arranges it with Black Chin Joe, or some such extraordinary character, to get the young man hanged. This duly happens, which, I gather, relates in some obscure way to the title. The fact remains that he is hanged with a length of rope, which to me suggests that the cover of the magazine could have been that of a hanging man.

This, in turn, might have formed the basis for a shadow. Unless one is an experienced artist it is not easy to draw a perfectly natural hanging figure, accurate enough to pass in silhouette as the real thing. I must trace this issue and see the cover. Then, I think, I shall have taken another big stride forward.

The time is 3.30 a.m.

Perfectly satisfied with herself to date, Maria returned the book to its position under her pillow and then, contrary to all she had told Pat, she went to sleep again. It was 7.30 when she awoke to sounds in the house.

She arrived downstairs to find each member of the family at breakfast. Pat made no reference to the matter of the magazine-borrowing in the night; and in any case her attitude towards her brother was such that she was hardly on speaking terms with him.

It being Sunday, and anxious to avoid questions Maria excused herself immediately after breakfast and went out for the day. She did not spend it uselessly, but made a note of all the likely places where magazines might be sold, which places she intended to visit on the morrow.

The following morning, Monday, she was again saved from having to say much by the fact that the Taylors were busy preparing to attend the funeral of Keith. Not being a mourner herself, Maria left the house early and drove into town.

Her first stop was at the covered

market in Redford's main street, a likely spot wherein to find American remainder magazines. She found such a stall at the far end of the big acreage and an elderly man with a bald head and walrus moustache watched her in puzzlement as she considered and turned over the disorder of magazines. Considering that the issue she sought was a year old, she realized her quest was pretty hopeless.

'Anythin' I can do, lady?' the stall-holder asked, puzzling at a middle-aged lady of obvious culture examining all sorts of magazines dealing with anything from the horrific to scantily clad glamour girls.

'Er — hmmm. I doubt it.' Maria fixed him with her cold blue eyes. 'However, if you happen to have a copy of *Super Crime Stories* — '

'Tons of 'em!' the stallholder interrupted eagerly. 'You can — '

'Kindly allow me to finish, my man. I require one particular issue — for June last year.'

'Oh . . . that won't be easy. I only buy up job lots — remainders. I never even looks at the date.'

'Quite so. Well — hmm — the issue in question may perhaps portray a hanging man. The story concerned is entitled — ' Maria sniffed slightly — 'entitled 'Swing It, Baby'.'

'Never 'eard of it,' said the stallholder helpfully. 'All the magazines I've got is 'ere, lady. 'Elp yourself.'

'Thank you for the invitation, but I have already done that without success . . . Good morning to you.'

Maria went on her way. Since there were no more magazine stalls in the market she marched outside, drove her car to an official park, and then began a deliberate ferreting, burrowing search into every likely shop and store she could find.

After each exploration she emerged again, sunshade in hand and her face revealing a deepening annoyance. By lunchtime, beaten for the time being, she retired to Maddison's Café and ordered a lunch.

And, whilst she sipped tea and considered the plaice and chipped potatoes on

212

the plate before her, Pulp Martin was in the midst of his own particular investigation, conducting it in his own weird and wonderful way.

He had, in fact, prepared much of the ground the evening previously, by making a round of the public houses. Not that he himself drank to any extent, but he figured that dustmen might — and the main thing was to find the dustmen who handled the bins from Cypress Avenue. Exploring from vault to vault, he had failed to track down the particular dustman in question, but he did learn his name. Joe 'Iggins. And Joe 'Iggins was liable to be at the 'tip' for some 'snap' around twelve today, Monday.

Pulp hazarded that 'snap' probably meant food — so whilst Maria ate her lunch, Pulp stood at the gates of the local destructor works yard, propping up one of the stone pillars. A yard overlooker informed him that Joe 'Iggins would be arriving soon on No 29 truck.

At ten past twelve No. 29 truck came in view, and Pulp straightened up. With absolute authority he held up his hand, stepped in the path of the truck, and waited. It stopped.

' 'Wot th' hall-fired blazes is the idea?' demanded the driver, his dirty face peering out from under a grey uniform-cap.

'You Joe 'Iggins, feller?' Pulp asked.

'No — 'e's sittin' on the back. An' you've no blasted right stoppin' me, neither.'

'Okay, pal, keep your shirt on,' Pulp advised; then he strode to the back of the truck where three men sat precariously on a ledge of wood amidst hanging sacks, shovels, and buckets. Three dirty faces looked at Pulp — probably in surprise. The dirt made it difficult for Pulp to be sure.

'Which of you guys is Joe 'Iggins?' he questioned, and a little man in the middle jumped down to the concrete.

'I am. What d'you want?'

'If you can spare a minute from this chariot I'll tell you.'

'All right; it's time for my snap, any road.' Joe' Iggins snatched at a tin box on the ledge and then yelled for the driver to

214

carry on. Turning, he looked at Pulp in plain wonder.

'I don't know you. What d'you want with me, anyway?'

'I figgered you might like to earn a few quid,' Pulp said.

'Don' what, mate? An' say, you're a Yank, ain't you?'

'Uh-huh — that makes us cousins . . . Now listen, I'm lookin' for a lamp, or some sort of lantern. It ain't a big one see, an' it ain't a little one neither. The sort of thing y'can stick a candle or a keros — paraffin lamp in. Now — '

'What's all this got to do with me?'

'For Pete's sake let me finish, can't you?' Pulp gave a glare. 'The lamp I'm lookin' for was probably tipped out with the refuse from eighteen Cypress Avenoo.'

'If it were,' the dustman said, 'I don't know nowt about it — an' I want to get my snap.'

'Ferget your belly for a minute, can't you, an' listen? This is urgent, see. I've got to find that lamp. Here — see if this'll put bubbles in your think-tank.'

Pulp handed over two pounds and the dustman reflected for a moment.

'I empty the bin at eighteen Cypress Avenue,' he said, but I don't remember nothin' about a lamp — '

'All right, so you don't remember. Supposin' there were one in the rubbish; where would it go?'

'On t'dump. 'Ere, I'll show you.'

Pulp nodded and strode beside the little dustman until they came to a wilderness of clinkers, ashes, and debris beyond the main destructor yard. Here there stood three magnetic cranes, motionless at the moment, their drivers squatting on the tractors and eating their mid-day sandwiches.

'There y'are,' the dustman said, pointing to one of the dumps. 'Look fer yourself. More'n I'd care to do. And watch out fer glass.'

'You wouldn't try foolin' me, would you?' Pulp asked sharply. 'If you've had that magnetic thing at work, the lamp may have bin lifted.'

'They 'aven't been workin' on that dump I've pointed out to you — an' won't till

Wednesday. Last week's muck's there, just as we tipped it.'

'Uh-huh,' Pulp acknowledged, scratching the back of his neck. Okay, I'll take a look.'

He did, mentally deciding that he was like a fly on a manure heap. The dustmen, seated at a distance, watched him and grinned among themselves. The sight of an overdressed Bowery thug ferreting amidst tin cans and clinkers was a new brand of entertainment for them.

'Crazy,' Joe 'Iggins observed, as he settled amongst his comrades with his tin box at his side. 'Ain't no other explanation. 'E gave me two quid so's he could look for an old lamp that's been chucked out of eighteen Cypress.'

The dustman next to Joe gave a sudden start and then reached behind him.

'Think 'e could mean this?' he asked, and by its hook he held out a lamp with black-painted glass sides, its framework livid in pillar-box red.

Joe nearly choked over his sandwich. ''Struth, that may be it! Where'd you get it?'

'Saw it on that dump where 'e is now. I was up in the crane then. Wondered what it were, lookin' so red like. It'll make a swell lamp for the kid's Christmas tree, dolled up a bit.'

'Blast your Christmas tree!' Joe said. 'This feller'll pay nearly anythin' fer this — half cut fer me since I interdooced him.'

The saviour of the lamp nodded. 'Done. Call 'im Joe.'

Hearing himself hailed, Pulp came slowly up the clinkery slope to where the four men were gathered. He was shown the lamp and his eyes gleamed.

'Yeah, I reckon that'll be it,' he agreed. 'Okay, Aladdin, hand it over.'

'Like 'ell,' Aladdin objected. 'Finder's keepers, or didn't y'know that?'

'A chiseller, huh?' Pulp's eyes narrowed. 'Okay, I'll pay. Can't blame a guy for tryin' to get it fer nothin'. How much?'

'Oh, say twenty pounds.'

Pulp swallowed something and the colour in his face became a shade deeper.

'You kiddin'?' he breathed. 'Twenty

pounds fer a broken-down lamp you found in the dump?'

'Ain't so broken-down. Fact that you want it puts a value on it. I 'appen to want it, too. I want payin' by way of compensation.'

'That lamp's under the headin' of salvage,' Pulp retorted. 'I'll give you five quid and no more.'

'Twenty!' Aladdin insisted.

Pulp glanced about him. The destructor works' main yard was quite a distance from there, and nobody was in sight. There were only these four men. Pulp nodded to himself, smiled, and then began to take off his jacket. He laid it carefully on the ground beside him and began to roll up his sleeves. Red thickly muscled forearms came into view and Aladdin began to shift uneasily.

'I reckon I don't know much about laws in this half-pint country,' Pulp said, grinning menacingly, 'but I do know when a guy is trying to gyp me. I've offered you five an' you want twenty. Okay, you get nothin' — an' this fer interest!'

His right fist bunched and whipped upwards. It hit Aladdin under the jaw and sent him flying backwards over the broad tractor belt, to collapse helplessly against the crane's bodywork, the lamp on his chest. Pulp snatched up the lamp and then whirled round as the three remaining dustmen descended upon him.

It was their first and last experience in dealing with a product of the Bowery. They did not know Pulp's nickname, otherwise they would have been aware that he had earned it through smashing jaws with his fists. He whirled, punched, side-stepped, upper-cutted — and left the remaining three dustmen grovelling in the cinders and spilled lunch-boxes.

'Been nice knowin' yer,' Pulp commented, and picking up his jacket he walked swiftly away, the lamp in his left hand.

'Mebby I shouldn't have acted up like that,' he reflected. 'Seem to remember there's somethin' in the law about assault — oh, what the heck! How c'n they find me? Anyway, I saved Maria a few quid

220

. . . Though what use this perishin' lamp is I'll be durned if I know.'

He inspected the lamp as he walked. It was all metal, square, with a ventilated top and base. In the base were holes, clogged with dirty candle-grease. The top had a hook for hanging purposes. The top was also smoky, especially inside the raised piece that acted as a chimney. The queerest thing about the lamp was that the glass sides, which slid into sockets, had been painted with black enamel. The slots themselves had microscopic holes.

'I don't get it,' Pulp muttered, scowling. 'What in blue thunder's the good of a lamp if it doesn't give a light? Screwy if you ask me.'

When he reached the main street in Redford he did a double-take — for the simple reason that he saw Maria's car on the park, the only car at the moment. The knowledgeable residents had picked the side streets.

With a grin Pulp ambled over to the Austin Seven and leaned against it to wait. The car park attendant's eyes narrowed suspiciously, and with good reason. Pulp was pretty dirty from his various activities, and the lamp dangling from his hand suggested doubts as to his sanity.

Finally the car park attendant came over, tossing down onto his chair the magazine he had been reading.

'What's the idea?' he asked curtly.

'Huh?' Pulp turned to him lazily. 'Oh, just waitin' fer somebody.'

'Then wait somewhere else. This car isn't yours.'

'I know it. Give a guy a chance, can't you? Wait till Black Maria shows up, then you'll see.'

The car-park attendant gave a start. 'A black maria, eh? So you're a jail-bird! I thought there was something funny about the way you — '

'You half-baked dope!' Pulp yelled. 'Black Maria's a dame — I mean a lady. See? Best little lady a runt like you ever clapped eyes on. You — '

'Upon my word, Mr. Martin, what have I done to merit such eulogy?'

Pulp swung round in surprise as Maria

came in view, sunshade firmly gripped in her hand. She was looking smiling and ample after her lunch.

'You know this bloke, lady?' the car park attendant demanded.

'Yes, certainly I do.' Maria's eyes strayed to the lamp. To the attendant she added, 'This gentleman is a very great friend of mine — and I can assure you that he is not nearly such a desperate character as he looks.'

'But — but he said somethin' about waiting for a black — maria! I don't want any trouble on this car park.'

'There won't be. I am Black Maria,' Maria said calmly, and gave a wicked smile.

'Oh . . . ' The man looked blank. 'Oh! Okay, then, I'll — I'll get back to my reading.'

He backed away uncertainly and reseated himself on his chair by the ticket office. By degrees he lost himself in his magazine again.

'Good job you came when you did, Maria,' Pulp muttered. 'Otherwise I guess I'd have beaten the pants off that guy.'

'Quite, Mr. Martin, but the matter is

no longer relevant. I observe that you have been successful in your search for the lamp.' Maria unlocked the car door. 'I must congratulate you most heartily.'

'Yeah, only I — I had to beat up four guys, Maria. They was aimin' to gyp me, and that meant gypping you, too, I figgered I didn't ought to stand for it.'

'Beat them up?' Maria repeated, startled. 'How badly?'

'Oh, I guess they'll live,' Pulp growled. 'Only I'm sort of jittery lest the law starts lookin' fer me. I'm allergic to cops, as I've told you before.'

'Tell me what happened,' Maria ordered, and Pulp did so. By the time he had finished Maria was smiling serenely. 'I am sure you have nothing to fear, Mr. Martin. I don't think dustmen are entitled to lift things — not openly that is — from a refuse dump. They won't say anything, and you did rightly to teach them honesty . . . Come into the car.'

Pulp nodded and slid into the seat next to the driving-wheel. Maria wheezed into position and slammed the door; then she took the lamp and examined it intently, regardless of the greasy dirt it left on her fingers.

'Evidently thrown away without the least effort being made to clean it,' she commented. 'You observe that a small stump of candle is still left?'

She had slid up one of the glass sides and was pointing inside the lamp.

'Look, Maria,' Pulp said, 'maybe it's the fact that I ain't had any lunch yet, but I can't seem to get the angle back of all this. What are you *driving* at? How'd this lamp come to kill Keith Robinson?'

Maria smiled a little. 'It didn't, Mr. Martin. It was, I think, one of the 'props' by which the 'suicide' effect was contrived.'

'How, f'rinstance?'

'You have asked a rather difficult question Mr. Martin,' she confessed, still studying the lamp. 'You see, the point is this: as I have already told you, the party of people at the house on the day of the 'suicide' saw the shadow of a hanging man.'

'Yeah, you told me that. So?'

'Pat Taylor told me that she thought the shadow was not clear cut round the edges, as far as she could remember. Possibly she hardly had the time to notice such a fact, but I am working on the assumption that she *did*, and I have followed out a theory from her statement. Had it been the genuine shadow of a man, it would have been clear-cut: no doubt of that. Since Pat seemed doubtful of the fact I have leaned to the possibility of a cut-out drawing of a hanging man, enlarged to life size by its distance from the wall — on which everybody saw the shadow — and consequently losing sharpness of outline because of magnification. The cut-out itself would be hidden by the curve of the stairway, since from the top of the cellar steps it is not possible to see the electric light — in front of which the cut-out would be placed. You follow me?'

'Yeah — so far. But that shadow must ha' been there when Keith went into the cellar, mustn't it?'

'*That* is the point!' Maria exclaimed. 'I do not believe the shadow was there at that moment.'

'It wasn't?' Pulp looked mystified.

'Then how the Sam Hill did it get there? You don't mean that Keith himself fixed it up somehow?'

'No, nothing of the kind. I believe,' Maria went on slowly, 'that the crime relied on timing. Perfect timing! I do not believe for one moment that the murderer would have risked letting Keith see that shadow because it might have meant that he would have dashed out of the cellar in alarm. In fact he would have done . . . so it had to be arranged that he didn't see the shadow, but everybody else did.'

Pulp sighed and scratched his head. 'No use, Maria; you got me stymied.'

'Then listen for a moment . . . The cut-out pattern of a hanging man could have been drawn up out of the way of the bulb, maybe held by a piece of thread or something. That Keith would look up towards the bulb was an unlikely possibility, and in any case I think it quite likely that by the time he reached the cellar a drug in his lemonade was taking effect, and he was on the verge of collapse. Timing again — notice? Now, if somehow the thread holding up the cut-out image were to be broken, the image would drop into position in front of the bulb . . . The image could have been hung on a pin, the pin being driven into the beam that crosses the ceiling in front of the bulb. The collapse of the thread holding the image *out of the way* brings this lamp into the picture, I think. If a piece of thread — cotton — were tied round the candle it would be burned through when the flame descended that far. Once again — timing!'

Pulp scratched the end of his nose. 'Yeah, I get the idea dimly, Maria, but I'd have to see it work to get the angle. It's too hazy as it is.'

'Even to me it is hazy,' Maria confessed. 'I know what I mean, but I find it unexpectedly difficult to put into words . . . All right, you shall have an actual demonstration and see what you make of it.'

'I thought I wasn't to come to the joint?'

'Tomorrow,' Maria answered, 'the entire family will be at business — Pat included — the last respects having been paid at today's funeral. I want you to come to the house tomorrow morning and we'll try and reconstruct things in the cellar . . . There will be Mrs. Taylor, of course, but she won't bother us in the least. She knows that I'm trying to find Keith's murderer, anyway.'

'Okay,' Pulp said. 'But look, isn't this dame Pat liable to get het up? You've let her in on everything so far, haven't you?'

'So far — but things are moving now in such a manner that I prefer to exclude her somewhat. She might tell everything back to her parents and brother — even to Ambrose Robinson — and that would make our task all the harder.'

'Yeah; probably would. And say — somebody must be one heck of an artist to draw a hanging figure good enough to look like one.'

'I observe you are as alert as ever, Mr. Martin,' Maria approved. 'That same thought occurred to me. The answer to that lies, I think, in a certain magazine owned by Gregory Taylor . . . ' She explained her theory of the vanished cover and added a few words to comment upon the failure of her search so far.

'A year back, huh?' Pulp mused. 'That won't be too easy, I reckon. *Super Crime Stories* . . . Yeah, I've read some of 'em. They stink. Ain't a bit like the real thing.'

'Hmm — that is hardly relevant. The fact remains I have to find that issue and take a look at the cover. It has become a missing link in the chain. I have been wondering if I might contact the American publishers and — '

Maria stopped dead. She was staring in fascination through the open side window of the car. Pulp's eyes followed her gaze across to where the car park attendant was lolling back in his chair as it tilted on its hind legs. The magazine he was reading had its cover visible in the bright sunshine. It was *Super Crime Stories* and the cover drawing was that of a hanging man . . .

'Cut off me hair and call me Baldy,' Pulp whispered. 'That's *it*!'

He snapped open the car door, scrambled out, and dived over to the attendant.

'How much for the cover of this mag,

feller?' Pulp stared at it avidly.

The attendant, already privately convinced that Pulp was an escaped lunatic, stared up at him blandly.

'For — for the *cover*?' he gulped. '*This* cover?'

'Aw heck!' Pulp snorted. 'Here's a quid. Gimme!'

He whipped up the magazine, tore the cover off, and then handed the magazine back. The attendant inspected it dazedly and watched as Pulp climbed back into the Austin and handed over his find.

'It has been truly said that the thing one needs most is right under one's nose,' Maria breathed. 'Excellent! Splendid! Ah — you observe this drawing?'

Pulp considered it. It portrayed a man hanging by a rope from a hook. The man occupied all the front cover and was shown in a sideways position. His hands were tied behind him — a fact that would not be evident in silhouette — and the cord from his neck went tautly upwards. His head was lolling slightly forward.

'I'll *swear* this is a duplicate of the cut-out which made the shadow on the cellar wall!' Maria declared, her eyes bright. 'I can hardly wait to make sure.'

'Kind of gives you butterflies in the belly,' Pulp agreed

'Quite so, Mr. Martin — even if the simile has a tendency towards the vulgar. However,' Maria put the cover in her handbag, 'we must remain patient. Tomorrow morning we will experiment — and, by the way, since you are likely to be engaged on a sooty job I would suggest you procure overalls from somewhere and put them in an attaché case. Don't let them be seen. Less revealed the better. You understand?'

'Yeah ... Anything else I should know?'

'There is a great deal more you should know, Mr. Martin but we will go into that some other time ... I shall not be needing you again until ten o'clock tomorrow morning at the Taylor joint.'

Pulp stared, but Maria kept her face straight and added, 'Here is your money to date, and your retainer fee.'

Pulp took it, grinned, and then squirmed out of the car.

'Thanks, Maria — and I'll see you tomorrow, with overalls. Now I guess I'll get a spot of mash and then hunt around for a chorus I can watch tonight.'

Maria switched on the ignition. 'Goodbye, Mr. Martin,' she said gravely, and drove at a sedate pace out of the car park.

11

Maria returned to the Taylor home, but instead of answering the questions posed for her she sidetracked them, and evinced an extraordinary interest in the funeral of Keith.

'The funeral's finished and done with and Keith has been put down,' Gregory Taylor said bluntly. 'I don't like saying it, Miss Black, but except for you he could rest in peace, and so could we. Why rake up so much dirt because of your theories?'

The evening meal over, the entire family was seated about the drawing room. Maria herself was in an easy chair, her elbows on the arms and her fingers interlaced. At Greg's outburst she gave a wintry smile.

'I must remind you, young man, that you yourself also suggested murder,' she said calmly. 'After mooting such a possibility you surely don't suggest that absolutely nothing should be done about it?'

'Well — no, but some things are best left alone if only for the sake of the people concerned . . . And anyway, you haven't found a thing yet which can be classed as proof, have you?'

'Whatever delay there may be is occasioned entirely by the cleverness of the murderer,' Maria answered, 'but I intend to remain here until I have proved my point. If you should wish me to leave I will do so, and hand over whatever information I have to the police. And I hardly need to remind you that if the police enter into it they will be utterly ruthless . . . As things stand I am refraining from telling them anything until — or unless — circumstances force me into it.'

'I'm not sure but what I wouldn't sooner have them here poking around than have you keeping us on edge,' Gregory said. 'At least they would tell us how far they're getting.'

'Perhaps,' Maria said, unperturbed. 'And certainly they would finally arrest the murderer. That is something I cannot do — so in that respect at least matters are perhaps best in my hands.'

Mr. Taylor looked across at Maria fixedly over his reading glasses. 'That sounds as though you are accusing one of us!' he exclaimed.

'Oh, don't be so silly, Harry!' Mrs. Taylor reproved him. 'We didn't have anything to do with it — except for Greg drugging the wine, that is. But then, that had nothing to do with the murder, had it?'

Mr. Taylor took off his glasses and polished them. Gregory remained silent and tight-lipped. On the hassock Pat stirred suddenly.

'What about old man Robinson?' she demanded. 'The most likely possibility of the lot, Miss Black, and you hardly seem to ever mention him! Why pick on us?'

'Only because I have every reason to,' Maria answered. 'One of the members of the celebration party murdered Keith, and it is only a question of time before I find out *which* one.'

'You think *I* did it, don't you?' Greg

demanded harshly, thumping the table. 'Those two girlfriends of Pat's had nothing to do with it, and you evidently think old Robinson didn't have, either. You think it was I who killed Keith! *Don't* you?'

'Was it?' Maria asked, levelly.

'No! Even supposing I had done it, do you think I'd be idiot enough to admit the fact?'

'If you had done it you might be *sensible* enough to admit it. That would save a great deal of needless trouble.'

'Oh, this is farcical!' Mr. Taylor declared. 'Since all of us had more or less equal opportunity any of us might have done it — even I, or you, my dear,' he added, glancing at his wife. 'Even Pat! One is as possible as the other.'

'True,' Maria admitted. 'The point is, though, was the impelling motive as strong in each individual instance?'

Silence. Gregory gave Maria a grim look; then he lighted a cigarette and sat back in his chair. Mr. Taylor began rubbing his glasses and his wife contemplated the darning she was doing. Pat moved again presently and her dark eyes fixed on Maria.

'Do you think — ' she began; but Maria raised a hand.

'I really think it would be best, Pat, if we said no more,' she said. 'This unhappy business can only be brought to a swift conclusion by the culprit confessing — otherwise it will go on, until every unwilling fact is brought to light. I am resolved on that.'

Pat gave a troubled smile. 'I wish now I hadn't said that I thought Keith was murdered,' she muttered.

'Why?' Maria frowned at her. 'Do you mean that you would prefer that his slayer remain undetected?'

'Yes, I do!' There was unexpected defiance in Pat's voice. 'I thought at that time that old Robinson was at the back of it and I wanted to go to any length to make him smart for the things he said to me! He called me a drunkard — or as good as — and lots of other things besides! Accused me of leading Keith astray. I never hated him so much as I did then . . . And I'll always hate him!

That was my main reason for asking you to do something . . . Instead I find you in my own family suspecting every one of them — you think the responsibility lies between Mother, Father, Greg, or me. All right, supposing it does? It wasn't done for viciousness — like in an ordinary murder — but for some good reason. I'm convinced of that!'

'The law does not consider that there is ever a good reason for murder, Pat,' Maria replied. 'And please, all of you, don't accept things too much at their face value . . . At this precise moment I am not suspecting anybody specifically. As for your remarks about Mr. Robinson, Pat, I never suspected that you could be so — vicious!'

Pat stared. 'Vicious? Because I wanted to get my own back? That's only human, isn't it?'

'When it comes to wanting to see a man accused of the murder of his own son it comes pretty close to *in*human. Frankly, I am most disagreeably surprised.'

Pat folded her arms and gave a petulant smile.

Maria said no more. She picked up a magazine from the table beside her . . . but for the rest of the evening she hardly read a word. As ever, she was thinking, fitting together relevant details and discarding others. Pat's revelation as to her reason for wanting matters investigated had come as a shock.

★   ★   ★

Maria did not add to her notes upon retiring: she preferred to await the outcome of her experiments with Pulp the following morning. She found when she arrived at the breakfast table that only Mrs. Taylor was present, and in spite of all that had happened the previous evening her good humour appeared intact.

'I think I ought to apologise for my family last night, Miss Black,' she said, handing Maria her plate. 'Their nerves were on edge. Doesn't get me that way, I'm glad to say. Just the same,' Mrs. Taylor continued, her smile fading a little, 'I'd like you to promise me something,

Miss Black. If my husband, or Pat, or Greg, did such an awful thing you won't tell the police, will you?'

'You mean you would prefer that murder should go unpunished, Mrs. Taylor?'

'Well, no, not exactly . . . ' Mrs. Taylor meditated. 'Murder shouldn't go unpunished, of course — ever; but when nobody knows it was murder, except those immediately concerned, or who did it, except perhaps you, why should you exert yourself to tell the law when they think it was suicide?'

Maria laid aside her knife and said nothing.

'What I mean is, murder is only a word,' Mrs. Taylor persisted. 'A horrible, ugly word. But there might be such a thing as killing somebody to save somebody else. A sort of backhanded self-defence. The law would call it murder, but it wouldn't really be that.'

'I think I know what you are trying to say, Mrs. Taylor,' Maria commented, 'but I am in no position to make promises. Incidentally, what do you mean exactly by 'self-defence'?'

'I . . . er . . . ' Mrs. Taylor hesitated. 'I was just thinking. If my husband, or Pat, or Greg did it, they might have done it as the best way to stop the marriage of a . . . a mentally unsound person. That is self-defence, in a way.'

'In that you can hardly include Pat. She had merely to refuse to marry Keith, not kill him . . . And whatever you say, or however you try and twist it round, it is still murder!' Maria's jaw set in a way that terrified her college pupils on occasions; then she relaxed again and shrugged. 'Though I cannot promise not to tell the police if I should discover anything in the family which demands exposure I do promise you that you will know all about it at the same time as everybody else.'

'That's all I need to know,' Mrs. Taylor said, satisfied. 'Then we can talk it over before you take any definite action. But I think you're quite wrong, you know. There isn't anybody in my family who'd ever do such a terrible thing.'

Maria said quietly: 'Believe me, Mrs. Taylor, I am doing all in my power to prove everybody in the family innocent

— just as much as I am trying to find the guilty one. Or hadn't that thought occurred to you?'

'As a matter of fact it hadn't,' Mrs. Taylor admitted. 'Seeing you poking around and asking so many questions, I naturally assumed that ... Well, of course, you have to find the innocent as well, haven't you?'

'It is a common practice,' Maria agreed dryly. 'And incidentally I feel my position here most keenly. I just cannot regard myself as a guest any longer — and I know I have outstayed my welcome. I'd be much happier if you'd allow me to pay for everything to date.'

'Pay!' Mrs. Taylor looked scandalized. 'When you're trying to find a murderer and clear us all of suspicion? I won't even hear of it!'

'Well ... as you wish. This morning,' Maria went on leading up to the subject by easy stages, 'I shall be making a further examination of the cellar. A young American will be helping me — a Mr. Martin.'

'Oh yes, Pat's told me about him! In

fact she seemed sorry that he wouldn't be staying here. But then we just haven't the room, have we?'

'He will be here at ten,' Maria said. 'Just for the morning. I mention it in case it should be you who opens the door to him.'

Maria saw to it, however, that she opened the door herself, and to this end she stationed herself at the drawing room window and remained there until she saw Pulp come striding energetically up the front path, an attaché case in his hand.

He grinned broadly as he stood in the porch.

'Hiya, Maria! All set?'

'You sound as though you are referring to a jelly, Mr. Martin. Come inside . . . Oh, Mrs. Taylor — this is Mr. Martin.'

'Hiya,' Pulp acknowledged, shaking hands. 'The mother of a dame like Pat sure sounds as though she oughta be a friend of mine.'

'Pardon?' Mrs. Taylor asked blankly.

Maria cleared her throat. 'Er — Mr. Martin, I think we should confine ourselves to the business on hand. If you are ready for the basement?'

'Yeah, sure.'

Maria excused herself for a moment and went upstairs to her room. She returned hugging a brown paper parcel and gave Pulp a nod as he lounged against the wall. Together they descended into the cellar and Pulp stood at the base of the steps, hands on hips, looking about him.

'Well, looks same as any other cellar to me,' he said. 'How are you makin' out with the Taylor crowd? Seems to me they can't exactly welcome you being on the prod.'

'The prod? Hmm — well, I must admit they do not take too kindly to my investigations — '

'A moment,' Pulp interrupted, and going up the steps he locked the door on the inside. He returned to Maria's side with a grin. 'Just in case we get interrupted,' he explained. 'Go on — you wus sayin'?'

'I would merely mention that I seem to be getting involved in interminable arguments with the Taylors.'

'Think one of 'em did it?'

'I am almost convinced of it — but I don't know which one. I have the feeling that there is a great deal going on between them. A kind of — er — 'passing of the buck'.'

Pulp nodded sympathetically. 'I get it. They got you behind the eight ball, huh?'

'The — ? I'm sure I don't know. However . . . ' Maria unwrapped the parcel she had brought and produced the lamp. Up to now it had been locked away in her suitcase. She also brought out a torch and the illustration of the hanging man, which illustration she had now carefully snipped out with scissors. She glanced at Pulp as he stood watching.

'As I warned you, Mr. Martin, there is dirty work to be done. In the chimney here to be exact. Plenty of soot. You brought the overalls?'

'Sure did.' He opened his attaché case and brought the overalls to view. He quickly scrambled into them, then tied a knot in each corner of his livid handkerchief and placed it over his head.

'Amazing!' Maria summed up, eyeing him; then she handed him the torch and lamp. 'I hope your size won't prevent you squeezing up into the chimney. If you *can* manage it I want you to hang this lamp on a fairly new upwardly bent nail, which you will see driven into the chimney.'

'Okay . . .' Pulp moved to the fireplace and began a fierce working movement with his broad shoulders. Since this pinned his arms he had to raise them over his head. Torch in one hand and lamp in the other, he extended himself gradually into the chimney.

'Done it?' Maria asked anxiously.

'Yeah, sure. It's wider'n you'd think, Maria.' Pulp's voice boomed oddly. 'There'd even be room if I had a pot belly. Okay, I've put the lamp on the nail. What's next?'

'You should be able to see a small hole in the wall — light shining through it from the cellar bulb — '

'Sure do,' Pulp agreed, after a moment.

'Good! I want you to notice carefully where that hole comes in relation to the lamp. When you have discovered that bring the lamp down again and show me.'

Pulp moved convulsively for a moment or two and then eased himself down by giving at the knees. At last he was free and, filthy with soot, he scrambled out into the cellar, clutching the lamp tightly in one hand. The torch he handed back.

'There!' he said. 'That hole in the wall comes directly opposite this part of the lamp.'

Maria examined the lamp carefully. The slotted frames designed to hold the glass sides were each drilled with tiny holes, presumably for ventilation. The position that Pulp had indicated was directly opposite one of these holes, about half way up the lamp.

'Be the same on the other side if the lamp was hung that way,' he said. 'Only two possible ways to hang it.'

'Mmm, yes indeed,' Maria murmured. 'A hole in the wall opposite one of the holes in the lamp-side. What does that suggest to you, Mr. Martin?'

'You got me,' he confessed, shrugging.

'Does it not suggest to you that perhaps a string or thread was passed through the hole in the wall, then through the hole in the lamp-side? The end of the thread would be tied to the burning candle inside the lamp — at some point predetermined on the candle. When the flame got that far the thread was automatically broken. The fumes, for even a candle makes a smell, would go up the chimney. The black sides would prevent any glow of light being cast.'

'Gettin' back to that cut-out idea again, huh?' Pulp asked.

'Exactly. Take a look at this . . . ' Maria held up the cut-out figure of the hanging man. 'Had I some glue I would have put this on a stiffer backing,' she said; 'but I think you will grasp the idea. You will notice that the 'rope' is left in as a straight length of paper.'

'Uh-huh. So?'

'Imagine a pin through the extreme end of this 'rope'. Put the pin in the beam crossing the ceiling there, in front of the light bulb, and let the picture hang . . . '

Pulp whirled the backless chair to him, stood on it, and reached to the limit to obey Maria's instructions. Under her directions he pinned the hanging man directly in front of the bulb. On the opposite whitewashed wall, visible from the head of the stairs, the illusion would have appeared complete.

Pulp stared at the wall. 'Bust me wide open if it don't look like the real thing — even the paper on the neck part lookin' like the rope.'

'Precisely,' Maria agreed. 'We haven't finished yet, though. That image can swing from side to side on the pin holding it, can it not? Like a pendulum?'

Pulp swung it experimentally. 'Sure can.'

'Very well, then. Imagine the thread I have spoken of being fastened to the foot end of the cut-out, the thread then being drawn towards that hole in the wall. The image would be drawn up horizontally until it became parallel with the beam. In consequence the shadow on the wall would cease to be evident . . . I believe such a cut-out was secured in that position, the thread which held it being fastened round the burning candle inside the lamp. By careful prior timing the thread, at a given moment, was burned through and the cut-out dropped into place in front of the bulb.'

'Yeah, that's right,' Pulp agreed wonderingly. 'An' everything fits in. The chimney would hide the lamp, and the blackened glass would hide the flame. Only thing that give it away were them grease splashes. Sure is a mechanical set-up all right, an' it looks like the right one. Yeah, even to that nail being a new one. I guess it must have been left in because whoever put it there figured nobody would ever look in the chimney.'

'Or else because it is driven in so firmly that it could not be removed without a good deal of noise. Noise echoes in a chimney, of course.'

Pulp reflected. 'Must have made plenty of noise when the nail was put in.'

'Yes indeed — but we may be sure the murderer would do the job when alone. There was time then to plan it out. Once the job was done it would have been difficult to arrange a suitable moment to extract the nail, so it was left there . . . Incidentally, I take it there is room to swing a hammer in the chimney?'

'Uh-huh, just about,' Pulp agreed.

'And you said it was not so narrow as I had imagined?'

'That's right. Until it gets a little way up — then it's got a bend which'd stop anybody . . . ' Pulp paused as he considered the beam across the ceiling.

'Mebby there ought still to be the original pin which had the cut-out on it,' he said.

'You can look — but I doubt it.'

Carefully though Pulp examined the beam, there was no sign of the original pin. He climbed down to the floor slowly and stood thinking.

'Look, Maria — see that staple? That was where the body was hung, wasn't it?'

'Just so.'

'Well, if the body did happen to be there — and this cut-out idea ain't really right — the *body* would cast a shadow in just the same position.'

'Naturally,' Maria assented. 'The murderer made sure of that fact. Where would be the point in a cut-out casting a shadow, if, hanging on the staple, a body could not possibly have done so?'

'Uh-huh, I get it.' Pulp handed the cut-out back to Maria and reflected further. 'There's still a lot o' things I don't seem to get,' he said. 'This guy Keith, it seems, came down into this cellar of his own free will, and even locked himself in.'

'That is so,' Maria agreed. 'I think the cut-out image was drawn up at the time, and the candle was burning in the lamp in the chimney.'

'But wouldn't he see the image drawn up on the beam with the thread?'

'Possibly — but once again the matter of timing enters into it. It is quite likely that before being able to examine the image — granting he ever even noticed it — he dropped unconscious because of a drug.'

'Yeah, you mentioned that before. I ain't quite clear on it.'

Maria smiled. 'A drug was first administered in port wine to see how long it took to operate on Keith's constitution. Everybody reacts in a different way to drug, you know.'

'How d'you know a drug was given in port wine?'

'I first deduced it — then Gregory Taylor confessed to being the culprit. He told me that he administered the drug in the belief that it would produce in Keith an apparent intoxification — but I think that the real reason was to find out exactly how long it took a given quantity of drug to work on a man of Keith's constitution. Once Gregory knew the time taken — and he would make a point of finding out from Pat when the actual collapse took place — he had a good working idea how long it would take on a second occasion. Whether there was drug or not in the corpse the doctor didn't try to find out. He had no reason to. Even if he had, drug is rapidly assimilated and no trace would have been evident. Even poison is extremely difficult to trace in a cadaver.'

'Yes, but it was lemonade this time!' Pulp objected. 'That ain't an intoxicant like wine.'

'A good point, Mr. Martin, but I do not believe that the slight intoxicant produced by one glass of port wine is even worth considering — that is, not by comparison with the effect of a drug . . . So, knowing beforehand the time taken, the murderer sent Keith into this cellar on some pretext or other, knowing that he could hardly have got here before the drug operated and knocked him into a complete stupor.'

'Mmmm. Then what?'

Maria continued: 'He was not, I do not think, hanging at all when the shadow was seen. He was lying unconscious in this cellar, out of sight of those at the top of the stairs. Even if he had collapsed on the stairs themselves his body would have rolled down and round the bend out of sight from the top.'

'Then who done it?' Pulp asked grimly.

'Apparently the first person who came down here,' Maria replied. 'Everything was beautifully arranged. All that had to be done was slip the clothes-rope from the wall about Keith's neck and hang it on that staple. The murderer had only to stand on the backless stool and leave it overturned as though Keith himself had kicked it over. Everything was to hand

— and Keith himself would be stupefied and unable to struggle . . . Then, whip away the paper image, pin, and thread, easily put in the pocket, and the thing was done. The lamp could be removed at leisure any time — and evidently was and thrown in the dustbin. The perfect crime.'

'But didn't the police come and look into things? How come they didn't see candle-fat splashing down into the grate? The lamp would still be burning, wouldn't it?'

'I hardly think the murderer would be that careless. The bit of candle we found was burnt out. I believe that the flame expired a few seconds after burning the thread — the thread being very close to the candle base, or even under the base itself. That would mean flame and thread would both cease to be almost simultaneously.'

'Yeah . . . And all the police would see would be candle-grease spots — if they saw 'em at all. A natural!' Pulp agreed. 'We only want to know who wus first down here and this case is all sewed up.'

'The first person down here was Mr.

Taylor senior,' Maria said quietly.

'So *he* did it, did he?'

'Apparently.' Maria gazed in front of her, pondering.

'But there ain't no doubt about it, surely?' Pulp persisted. 'You've got this whole thing worked out an' — '

'There are still some outstanding points,' Maria' interposed. 'I know that it all points to one thing — that Taylor senior came down here first, was left alone for a few minutes whilst Gregory telephoned for police and doctor — during which time Taylor could have hanged the stupefied Keith. But there is also the fact that Gregory admits it was he who drugged the wine.'

'Then mebby they wus in on it together — else Greg is tryin' to shield his pop.'

'Gregory is also the one with a knowledge of criminal methods,' Maria pointed out. 'Besides that, he is the owner of the magazines from which I am sure the hanging man was cut out . . . I have to decide where Gregory fits into this, Mr. Martin, and also if Mr. Taylor is really guilty.'

'Why don't you tell the police an' let 'em grill him?'

'Grilling is not a procedure which is adopted over here, Mr. Martin — and in some cases it is perhaps a pity . . . ' Maria put the lamp, torch, and cutting back into the brown paper parcel. 'I think we have done all we need here. You will find a water tap over there. Just wash yourself and then we will return upstairs.'

He nodded, jammed the overalls in his attaché case, and then went over to the tap. He dried his face and hands on his handkerchief and then followed Maria to the upper regions. Glancing into the drawing room, they found Mrs. Taylor tidying it up.

'Finished?' she enquired, switching off the whining vacuum.

'We have made an extensive survey,' Maria responded. 'And I think it would help if you say nothing to the rest of the family. They will ask questions which it would be tedious to answer.'

'All right,' Mrs. Taylor agreed, shrugging. 'If it makes for peace I won't say a word.'

Maria nodded and turned to Pulp. 'I shan't be needing you any further at the moment, Mr. Martin. Remain in Redford, and when I want you I'll get in touch with you there.'

'Okay, Maria. Be seeing you, Mrs. Taylor.'

Mrs. Taylor looked after him with a puzzled stare, and after a moment the front door closed behind him. Maria wandered into the drawing room slowly and set her brown parcel on the floor beside her chair as she seated herself.

She looked across at Mrs. Taylor as she busied herself with dusting. 'Mrs. Taylor, when the shadow of Keith's hanging body was seen on the cellar wall I believe your husband stopped any of you going into the cellar and instead cleared the hall, telling your son to go and 'phone for police and doctor. Is that right?'

'Quite right. We said that in court, if you remember.'

'I just wanted you to verify it. And your husband was the first person to go and make an attempt to cut down the body?'

'That's right. As it happened he

259

couldn't manage it single-handed and Greg had to help him. But of course it was too late by then and Keith was dead.'

Maria fondled her watch-chain. 'If you don't mind, Mrs. Taylor, I would like to reconstruct the time when Keith was first found to have disappeared from this room. Pat was the first to notice the fact, was she not?'

'Yes,' Mrs. Taylor assented, 'and she went to look for him and couldn't find him. Then Mr. Robinson had a look round too in case Keith had gone . . . er . . . well, upstairs. Being a man . . . But he couldn't find him either. Then we all started to look and found the cellar door locked on the inside and . . . and that was that.'

'And Mr. Taylor *was* the first to go down and inspect the body?'

'Yes.' Mrs. Taylor frowned. 'But why do you keep insisting on it? What has that got to do with it?'

'So much — so much,' Maria muttered. 'You see, Mrs. Taylor, I . . . ' She paused and got to her feet. 'Pardon me a moment; a thought just occurs to me.'

She went out into the hall and opened the cellar door, examining the lock carefully — more so than she had on the first occasion — and then the key. From a pocket of her dress she took a small but powerful folding lens and studied the key through it.

Upon the end of it were scratches moving in circles, conforming to the roundness of the key stem. Maria smiled faintly as she put the key back in its hole . . . Behind her in the drawing room the vacuum was buzzing again — but Mrs. Taylor was not operating it. Maria re-entered the room to find her staring at the contents of the brown paper parcel that had been beside the chair.

'You find my goods and chattels interesting?' Maria asked.

'Oh! I — I'm so sorry, Miss Black. I was going to lift this parcel of yours on to the table so I could vacuum the floor, and the paper fell apart. No string round it.'

'No, no string round it,' Maria agreed, her eyes frosty.

'Where,' Mrs. Taylor asked slowly, 'did you get that lamp from?'

'After a good deal of searching I obtained it — or rather Mr. Martin did — from the local destructor works. Why?'

'It's just like one Greg keeps in the garage. He uses it in the winter with an oil lamp in, to do odd jobs . . . And this picture you've cut out! A hanging man! What's it for?'

Maria hesitated and then swung round as a key grated in the front door lock. A second later Gregory came in view. He paused in the act of uttering a greeting to stare at the stuff on the floor. A look of genuine blank surprise crossed his face.

'Say, where on earth did this come from?' He picked up the lamp and examined it.

Maria considered him. 'I take it that it is yours?'

'Yes, of course it is. I keep it in the garage as a rule — pretty useful in winter weather. But who painted these glass sides with black enamel? It'll take me hours to get it off.'

'It came from the destructor works,' Maria answered. 'It got there by way of the dustbin in the garden.'

'*Our* dustbin?' Gregory frowned. He put the lamp back slowly on the brown paper. 'Who does this parcel belong to, anyway?'

Mrs. Taylor nodded towards Maria.

'I — I'm sorry, Miss Black,' Gregory apologized. 'I didn't know it was yours. Only it being my lamp . . . And this too!' He looked at the cut-out of the hanging man. 'I could swear that picture is from the cover of one of my magazines.'

'The cover that you complained of having lost?' Maria enquired.

'Yes, that's right.' Gregory's eyes narrowed. 'It *is* the cover scene. I remember it clearly. Where did you find this lost cover of mine?'

'It is a duplicate of it, Mr. Taylor — not the one you lost. Where I got it does not signify.'

Maria left Gregory wrestling with this remark and neatly made the parcel up again. With it cradled in her arm she looked at him.

'If you've come home for lunch, Mr. Taylor, you'd better not waste any more time . . . I shall be going out,' Maria added to Mrs. Taylor, 'and I am not quite sure when I shall be back.'

'Just as you like, Miss Black.'

Maria left the room, conscious of two pairs of eyes watching her fixedly.

12

Pat, working in her restaurant, was quite surprised when towards quarter to one the massive figure of Maria, entered, sunshade gripped in her hand and her hat set squarely on her severe hair-do. Maria paused for a moment by the doors, and then advanced to the cash desk.

'This is a surprise, Miss Black!' Pat exclaimed.

Maria smiled blandly. 'It shouldn't be — I need to eat sometimes, my dear. I have also another purpose in being here. If you can spare a moment I'd like a word with you.'

Pat glanced up at the big clock. 'I can manage it in about ten minutes. I'll get someone to relieve me. Take that table over there in the corner. It's where I always lunch — and it's quiet.'

Maria turned with solemn dignity and settled herself at the corner table. She gave her order to a laconic waitress and then sat back and reflected.

'How necessary it is to examine every aspect,' she muttered, staring into space. 'Otherwise one might quite easily leap at the obvious. Hmmm ... Fortunate, indeed that Gregory confessed to drugging the wine, otherwise I might have made a very serious mistake. Yes, indeed; one cannot be too thorough.'

Her mind went back over every detail of the moves she had made during the morning, from the moment Pulp had hung the lamp in the chimney to Gregory's look of supreme astonishment at finding the lamp with its glass sides blacked out.

'Definitely a surprise,' Maria mused. 'There is not the slightest doubt that that young man was surprised.'

Her reflections ceased as the waitress lowered a plate of steak pudding — so called — and chipped potatoes.

'I think I should remark, madam, that this is a staff table. You'd be more comfortable in the restaurant itself — '

'I am perfectly comfortable here, thank you, and I will have my tea now, with the meal.'

Beaten, the waitress retired. The tea was brought and Maria had just poured it and was studying the pseudo-steak pudding doubtfully when Pat came and settled at the opposite side of the table. A great light dawned across the square face of the watching waitress and she turned and vanished in the kitchen regions.

'I've managed to wangle it so I can have my lunch a bit earlier than usual,' Pat said. 'It'll give us plenty of time to talk.'

'Splendid!' Maria said. 'I find it necessary to ask a few more questions about Keith.'

'Oh?' Pat looked surprised. 'But didn't I tell you everything that could possibly matter?'

'Everything which was relevant at the time, no doubt, but now there are other facts which I would like to get. For instance, did he ever at any time mention any relatives, excluding his father, of course?'

Pat started to shake her head; then she hesitated and reflected instead. Her lunch had been brought by the time she was ready to answer.

'Yes, he did once. An aunt Lydia.'

'Mmm. On his father's or mother's side?'

'That I don't know.' Pat picked up her knife and fork. 'I seem to recall that he just referred to 'Aunt Lydia'. I never met her.'

Maria munched contentedly. Then, 'Did he ever mention where this aunt lives?'

'Yes. In Kingsford, the next town to this one. It's about fifteen miles away. Keith seemed to think pretty well of her from what he said . . . ' A frown crossed Pat's face. 'Come to think of it, it's rather odd really. Why wasn't she asked to the engagement party? It's a good job she wasn't as things turned out, of course, but that doesn't alter the fact that she wasn't even asked. I told Keith to ask everybody near to him — and Dad told Mr. Robinson the same thing. She wasn't at the funeral, either.'

Maria studied the chipped potato on her fork.

'There is, of course, the possibility that this relative was estranged, and did not wish to be mixed up with Keith, or his father. However, my problem is to find out exactly where this aunt lives.'

'What on earth for?' Pat asked in amazement.

'I am still not satisfied with all I have heard about Keith — views limited to yourself, your family, and Mr. Robinson. I'd like a direct outside opinion of Keith for a change.'

'Oh, I see. And you think that would help things?'

'Very much. You are sure you don't know where I can find her?'

'Sorry. All I know is that she lives in Kingsford.'

'Let me think now,' Maria mused. 'You don't know whether or not she is married, I suppose?'

'Keith never said.' Pat smiled a little. 'Somehow, though, 'Aunt Lydia' sounds dreadfully maiden-auntish.'

'Since Keith, you say, was apparently well disposed towards her, whilst not at all enamoured of his father, it is likely that Aunt Lydia is on the mother's side.'

'Yes, it's possible,' Pat admitted. 'But

we don't know Keith's mother's maiden name.'

'That I can get from the records at Somerset House,' Maria said; 'and I will, immediately after lunch.'

'You're going to an enormous amount of trouble to find this relative, aren't you, Miss Black?'

Maria smiled. 'I often go to an enormous amount of trouble to satisfy myself over a point. I believe in being thorough ... Really, these chipped potatoes are excellent! As to the steak pudding, I fancy it came out of the nearest tin.'

Pat hesitated before asking another question.

'Do you honestly believe, Miss Black, that either Dad, Greg, or Mother settled Keith? It's a horrible thought to keep having on my mind. I wish you'd ease things for me.'

'At the moment, Pat, that is not possible,' Maria answered. 'I think it by far the best thing if we dropped the subject.'

Thereafter Maria did not refer to Keith

again during the rest of the lunch. After it was over she bade Pat a smiling farewell and left the restaurant, walking resolutely towards the railway station. Her car, for the time being, she had left on the central park — to the deep suspicion of the magazine-reading attendant . . .

★ ★ ★

At 2.50 she was alighting at the station in London. At 4.00 she was once more in the station, and by 5.00 she was leaving the train at Kingsford, one station beyond Redford.

'Miss Lydia Baxter,' she murmured, as she went through the station exit. 'Hmmm — first let us see if the lady is listed as having a telephone.'

Maria managed to obtain a town directory at the public library ten minutes before closing time, and though the issue was three years old, Lydia Baxter was listed at 45 Olive Avenue. With a war-like look in her pale blue eyes, Maria emerged from the library and considered how best to find Olive Avenue.

Her inner worry, that Lydia Baxter might have married and so changed her surname, had gone now. Whilst at Somerset House Maria had considered investigating the records for the marriage of a Lydia Baxter, until she had thought of the thousands of married Lydia Baxters, and accordingly changed her mind. Her hunch that Lydia Baxter was a maiden aunt had been proven correct.

'Oh, my man!' Maria raised her hand at a street cleaner and he paused in his indolent brushing as she moved towards him. 'Where do I find Olive Avenue?'

'Other end of town, lady — about three miles away. A thirteen bus from 'cross the street'll take you right there.'

'Splendid!' And with sunshade firmly in her grasp — and regret in her heart that she had not stopped at Redford and picked up her faithful Austin Seven — Maria marched across to the stop.

Before very long the bus arrived and bore her swiftly to her destination. No. 45 Olive Avenue was a semi-detached stucco-fronted villa; the whole avenue reeked of conservatism and intense propriety. Every window had lace curtains, every window sill was spotlessly clean. All the front doors were highly polished.

Maria opened the wooden gate of No. 45, closed it, and stalked up the pathway, jabbing her thumb on the doorbell. Long pause, a bobbing shadow behind the stained glass of the door — then a woman came in view, peering as though she had emerged from a dark room to look out on the world.

'Yes?' Her extreme gentility made her almost inaudible.

'Will you be Miss Lydia Baxter?' Maria asked, using her most impressive smile.

'Yes,' the woman whispered.

'Er — splendid. I wonder if I could speak with you for a moment? It concerns the late Keith Robinson.'

'Keith . . . Poor Keith!' Miss Baxter pushed a wisp of stringy brown hair from her forehead and sighed. 'Please come in.'

Maria nodded and swept into a narrow, immaculate hall — then she obeyed directions and went into a drawing room to settle down. Everything about the room was old-fashioned.

''Arsenic and Old Lace',' Maria murmured to herself — and then she beamed upon the slight, bony wispy-haired, muttering Miss Baxter as she folded up on a low-built Jacobean chair.

'Keith . . . ' she repeated absently. Then in a far-away voice, 'What about him?'

Maria edged forward on her chair. 'My name is Miss Black, Miss Baxter,' she said. 'I must apologize for calling upon you in this fashion. You are of course, aware of the unhappy demise of Keith Robinson?'

'Oh yes. I read all about it.'

'You did not, however, attend your nephew's funeral?'

'I would not have done so even had I been asked. And I was not.' The voice rose a little. 'But what has all this to do with you, Miss — er — Black? Did you know Keith?'

'No; but I am a friend of the Taylor family. Keith was engaged to Miss Taylor, you know.'

'Yes; I read about that in the paper, too. But why should your friendship with the

Taylor family bring you here to ask me about Keith?'

Maria fingered her watch-chain as she considered.

'Perhaps it would be better if I made things a little more clear to you. I am an — er — investigator from the World Wide Assurance Company. There is a matter of insurance connected with Keith Robinson's death, and we are anxious to secure as many details as possible about him.'

Maria fervently hoped that this faded, inaudible lady in her highly select cocoon would not ask for credentials. She did not. She merely sighed.

'Poor Keith,' she said again, regretfully.

Maria moved impatiently. 'You are, I understand, the sister of Keith's mother, who died in the Sunbeam Home of Rest?'

'Yes, I am.' A stony look crept on to the pale face and it remained there.

'What can you tell me about Mrs. Robinson?' Maria asked.

'Evelyn? Well, nothing very much — except that she was one of the purest women who ever walked this earth.'

Maria cleared her throat. 'Er — You

may be aware from the court proceedings reported in the paper that Keith Robinson was assumed to have committed suicide whilst of unsound mind — attributed to inheritance of insanity from his mother — '

'Horrible, beastly lies!' Miss Baxter became emotional. 'Whatever her mental trouble when she entered the Sunbeam Home of Rest, she certainly did not have it in her youth. She was one of the brightest, happiest people one could meet.'

'I see . . . Then tell me, Miss Baxter, what brought about her — malady?'

It seemed strange to see a cold, sneering smile on the face of the gentlewoman.

'That husband of hers!' she retorted. 'Him and his psalm-singing and his eternal calling on the Lord. Rank, vile blasphemy! Nothing else!'

Maria smiled reflectively. 'I have heard the gentleman — er — hold forth. I never knew a man with such an extensive knowledge of the Scriptures.'

'It's a pity he doesn't imbibe the one

about 'taking the name of the Lord in vain . . . ' For he *does* — in all conscience he does!' Miss Baxter stopped to draw breath and then started off again. 'Believe it or not, Miss Black, when my sister was first married to him she was a happy, gentle soul — very much like me in type. Both of us had a respectable, even straitlaced, upbringing in refined sur- roundings. For a reason that I never understood Evelyn fell completely in love with Ambrose Robinson. She met him first at a dance and from then on nothing would satisfy her but that she marry him . . . '

Miss Baxter paused, frowned, and fixed her eyes on Maria. 'I wonder,' she asked, 'why I am telling you all this?'

'It cannot do any harm,' Maria replied, shrugging, 'and I am sure you find it a relief to be able to talk to somebody who understands.'

'Yes — that's right. It can't do any harm, can it?' Miss Baxter gave a slow, wistful smile. 'Well, Evelyn married him — though our parents did not like him, and neither did I. In fact I always used to find an excuse to avoid going to see Evelyn in case I met Ambrose. Instead she used to come and see me. Each time she came I couldn't help noticing that she was different — strange in manner, wondering, even downright vague. From little hints I picked up I gathered that Ambrose treated her abominably. Not in the legal sense, mind you, or I would have acted on Evelyn's behalf and have had the law deal with him . . .

'The devilish cunning of the thing seemed to be in what Ambrose did not do — his subtle innuendoes, his everlasting prating of the Scriptures, his parsimonious way of living, his utter miserliness. He crushed Evelyn's spirit. He broke her mind. I shall never cease to wonder that she survived the birth of Keith, for at that time she was in a terribly run-down condition, mentally and physically.'

Miss Baxter made a movement as though she felt the subject was becoming intolerable to her.

'After Keith's birth I saw little of her — and what I did see I didn't like. In some things she had become almost childish; in others completely absent-minded. I think an incessant concussion of shocks had left her bemused. I heard that Ambrose had had a doctor to see her, then to my horror I learned that she had been admitted to the Sunbeam Home of Rest. There ... she died. And I shall never cease to believe that it was Ambrose who hounded her into her grave.'

'According to the records,' Maria said slowly, 'your sister was mentally unbalanced when Keith was born — hence the assumption that Keith could have inherited her weakness.'

'No doubt he could,' Miss Baxter agreed, her voice sinking back into its normal quietness, 'but I am sure it was only Ambrose who brought on that unbalanced condition. There is no trace of insanity in our family, as far back as can be found. I made a point of investigating when I knew what had happened to Evelyn. Therefore I say that it was a condition forced upon her by that Bible-reading hypocrite she married. I never think of him, Miss Black, except with unspeakable loathing.'

'I understand,' Maria said, 'that seven years elapsed after Keith's birth before your sister was committed to the Sunbeam Home? You say that in that seven years she became progressively worse?'

'Yes. I begged and pleaded with her to let me have the real facts about life with Ambrose, but she never revealed anything — perhaps through a mistaken sense of loyalty. In face of that there was nothing I could do. I — I felt as though I were watching her drown and doing nothing about it.'

Maria got to her feet and laid a gentle hand on Miss Baxter's shoulder.

'You have my deepest sympathy,' she said quietly. 'And you may rest assured that all you have told me will not go any further — no, no, please do not trouble to get up.'

The woman rose, nevertheless, her tired, half-hidden eyes searching Maria's dogged face.

'Surely, Miss Black, you'll stay to have a cup of tea? So few people come to see me. I am almost a recluse. You're somehow so different from other women I have met — more commanding, more assured. You know where you're going . . . '

Maria smiled. 'I find your mention of tea irresistíble, Miss Baxter. Thank you so much. Yes, I will stay a little while longer.'

With an eager nod Miss Baxter fussed out of the room. Maria looked after her and reflected. ''Know where I'm going . . .'' she repeated slowly. 'Yes, I believe I do — at last.'

★   ★   ★

When Pat left the restaurant that evening she was surprised to find Gregory waiting for her in the street outside.

'There's something I need to talk over with you right away,' he said. 'Let's have some tea at that rival teashop across the road.'

Pat nodded. There was an urgency in her brother's manner which she had never seen before; but because she knew him so well she did not waste time asking questions.

'Something,' he said, when they were seated at a quiet table in Maddison's, with tea and cakes before them, 'has got to be done about Miss Black, and quickly! She's got to be made to clear out, and stay out.'

'That all?' Pat smiled as she poured out tea. 'Ever tried moving a mountain, Greg? Be easier than moving Black Maria! Don't forget she was my headmistress once and I know what she's like when her mind's made up.'

Gregory's light grey eyes glinted.

'You know who murdered Keith, don't you?' he asked, his voice low.

'I was hoping you wouldn't ever ask me that, Greg.' Anxiety clouded Pat's features. 'I just don't want to say it, but it couldn't have been anybody else but you, could it? You drugged that wine; you understand all about criminals; you've a good knowledge of law. I made up my mind to the horrible truth long ago and I've tried to sweeten the bitter fact by thinking you did it to save me from making a mess of my life.'

'You're completely wrong,' Gregory said evenly. 'I didn't even touch Keith, though I admit I'd have liked to. It was

Dad! What is more, a few steps further will bring Miss Black to *knowing* it was Dad, and then the fat will really be in the fire!'

'Dad?' Pat whispered, aghast. 'Oh no, Greg, you're utterly wrong! He'd never — '

'But I would?' Gregory asked sourly. 'Well, thanks for the sisterly affection.'

'I didn't mean it in that sense,' Pat protested. 'You often said you hated the idea of my marrying Keith — and to my mind that gave me reason for thinking you had a motive. Then when the wine business came up and you confessed to it — '

'You don't suppose that I really drugged that wine, do you? I only confessed to it because I felt convinced that Dad was the culprit. I also realized that if he tried to alibi his way out of it in that clumsy way of his he'd get into the most awful mess. So I took the blame to satisfy that confounded old busybody of a Miss Black as to what was wrong with Keith's wine, and so stop her investigating further about the drug, and also because I felt that with legal knowledge, as well as knowing what I do about the methods of criminals, I might be able to fence with Miss Black far more efficiently than Dad ever could. The fact remains that I did not drug that wine, and I'm quite sure you or Mum didn't because that just wouldn't make sense. So it leaves only Dad.'

'Have you . . . asked him?' Pat asked quietly.

'No. Nor do I intend to. If he wants to admit it, all right. If not, I shan't say a word. He knows perfectly well that I am on his side by my taking the blame for the drugged wine . . . But the time has come when this game is liable to get dangerous. Miss Black is moving far too fast for comfort . . . '

'What makes you think so?'

'I got home much earlier than usual for lunch this morning — to find that she had unearthed my lamp from the destructor works. It had been taken there in our dustbin. I never put it there, so Dad must have. The lamp's sides were all blacked out. From Mum I learned that Miss Black and that American pal of hers had spent the morning doing something in the cellar . . . Besides the lamp there was a cut-out figure of a hanging man, lifted from a cover duplicating the cover I lost from one of my magazines. Remember I played hell about it?'

'I'm not likely to forget it,' Pat retorted. 'As for the lamp, Miss Black was looking for it long ago. I helped her to do so — '

'You did, eh?' Gregory's eyes sharpened. 'Naturally, I have known for some time that Dad might have had something to do with Keith's death — '

'But how could you know?'

'I heard part of what he said to Keith,' Gregory answered calmly. 'I was quite near to him. He told Keith to go into the cellar because there was a surprise down there waiting for him . . . There was some more, but I didn't catch it. Maybe it was telling him to lock the door. Dad sent Keith into the cellar. That's why I'm so sure of Dad's guilt. On top of that, when I saw that cut-out image and lantern which Miss Black had got I knew how the whole thing had been engineered.'

'How?' Pat whispered.

'Amongst my magazines, there's a story called the 'Hanging Shadow', and the circumstances in it are identical to those which I think Dad used . . . Dad isn't the type to think up an ingenious crime all on his own. In fact very few crimes are original: invariably they are copies or improvised versions of crimes which have been previously committed. In this particular business of Keith we happened to have a cellar, a chimney, an electric light, and a curving staircase, all of which were also given in the story. Dad must have read that story at some time and got the idea from it.'

'*What* idea?' Pat demanded.

'In the story the image of a hanging man was cut out of cardboard, even to the rope round his neck, and the end of the 'rope' was pinned to a beam directly in front of the light. The feet of the image were pulled up so that the image lay in a horizontal position. This was done with a length of cotton that in turn was fastened round a candle inside a lamp. When the candle burned down far enough the cotton was severed and the shadow dropped in position on the opposite wall, the shadow being cast by the light at the back of it . . . I don't remember the rest of the story, and it doesn't matter, anyway. I'm sure Dad used that idea, and therefore used my lamp and pinched a suitable cover from one of my magazines to get an image in silhouette of a hanging man. And it was that cut-out shadow which we all saw from the top of the cellar steps.'

'Yes, it does look as though you must be right,' Pat admitted despondently. 'Miss Black has been keenly interested in the cellar chimney — and she even had me exploring the inside of it. I found a new nail on which the lamp could have been hung.'

'I saw it, too, this lunch-hour when I looked for myself,' Gregory said.

'Then just how did Keith get mixed up in the business?'

'It seems plain enough now,' Gregory answered. 'I've told you how Dad sent Keith into the cellar, and presumably, because he had been told to, Keith locked the cellar door after him . . . But he had been drugged. Dad knew — from making an earlier test on the wine — just how long that drug ought to take to have an effect. Keith collapsed, and if it was on the staircase he would have rolled down out of sight from the top. By the time we went to look for him the shadow was in position. Everything could be figured out beforehand by simple calculation. Dad went down *first*: that's the important thing . . . '

Pat sat listening with an expression approaching horror on her face.

'It was essential that he be first,' her brother went on, relentlessly. 'He chose a time when all of you were overwhelmed with the shock and I'd gone to ring for the police and doctor. When I reached him he was apparently trying to cut the body down. Actually, I think he had only just strung it up, but of course he had removed the paper image and thread. The lamp he could have taken out at any time, since it was hidden in the chimney. Being blacked out, the flame, if there was one, did not give it away.'

'It was the grease spots in the grate

which gave it away,' Pat said.

'I thought so. I noticed them particularly this lunch-hour, though never before.' Gregory drank his tea and gazed absently across the café.

'It's all so unspeakably horrible!' Pat breathed. 'And it seems to be likely that you have the right answer . . . Last night I found Miss Black searching through your magazines.'

Gregory gave her a sharp look. 'That simply makes things all the blacker,' he said. 'She was probably looking for the story which the missing cover picture had represented. From reading it she'd guess the cover, and the set-up. In fact she must have guessed the set-up before reading the story . . . I tell you, Pat, that woman's dangerous. She's got to be stopped, or the game's up, as far as Dad is concerned.'

'Can't you find some legal way to stop her?' Pat demanded.

'Possibly — but she's already said that if she quits she will tell the police all she knows; then Dad would be in a worse position than ever. The police would never show the restraint Miss Black uses.

No, that isn't the way to do it . . . '

'I just can't imagine Dad doing such a thing,' Pat said. 'Why *did* he? And suppose something had happened to go wrong with his timing and the stunt hadn't come off?'

Gregory shrugged. 'There wouldn't have been any damage done. Had the shadow not dropped on time, Dad would still have made sure that he went into the cellar first: he had the authority to do so in his own house. He would have quickly moved the cut-out and told us to come and have a look at Keith, who had apparently fainted. Later, perhaps, he would have tried again . . . But that didn't happen! Everything went according to plan. There was the rope to hand in the cellar, the backless chair, everything. Remember that Dad took Keith in the cellar with him on the night he went for the wine. Why? Not only to talk to him — as he said — but to provide for the inquest the fact that Keith knew, or could have known, that there was a rope and something to stand on in the cellar. If he had not had the chance to see them beforehand the whole plot would have fallen to bits . . . Everything was perfectly thought out, and it fooled the police and the coroner.'

'And he committed this terrible crime in order to save me?' Pat asked.

'Yes,' Gregory answered, without hesitation, 'because he isn't the kind of man to take such a risk — or commit such a crime — otherwise. Since you are over age he had no power to stop you marrying Keith, and nothing short of the removal of Keith *would* have stopped it. That's right, isn't it?'

'Yes, it's right,' Pat confessed in a low tone.

'Well, then, I think Dad must have discovered somehow that Keith was mentally peculiar, and to save you from marrying him and perhaps having a hell made of your future life, he took a chance on committing an outlandish but perfect crime. It worked, and by now it would be done and finished with except for your crazy idea of keeping Miss Black on after the crime was discovered. It was a fatal mistake. The way she figured out that

Keith wouldn't commit suicide with a clothes-rope, and that his writing was that of a mentally unstable person, was a darned good bit of criminology, I'll admit. Since she began poking round she's never stopped, but she's got to be, somehow.'

'I recall,' Pat said, thinking, 'that you too weren't so backward in saying that it was murder. If you'd stuck to the notion of suicide Miss Black might have given up the idea in the finish as being just a theory. Your verification made her doubly active.'

Gregory sighed. 'I did it chiefly to find out how much she had learned so far. She told us quite a lot, too, enough to confirm my private opinion that one of us was responsible — and that to me meant Dad.'

'Then it's his duty to confess.' Pat pushed away her teacup. 'Even if he is our father. Of course he won't say a thing, though he must know that you have guessed the truth. I'm sure he must have done it to protect me, so in return I'll protect him by saying nothing.'

'You'll do more than that,' Gregory said. 'You'll get Miss Black to pack up her traps and clear out.'

'I can't see her doing it!'

'She's got to! If you don't get rid of her I shall. Be better for you to do it if you can, though. My methods would be more effective — but far more dangerous. Either way, she must go! Now let's get back home and see what we can do.'

13

To the irritation of Pat, and almost the fury of Gregory, Maria did not return home during the evening: she was enjoying herself far too much discussing a multitude of topics with the whispering Miss Baxter in Kingsford.

Pat and Gregory both found it hard to appear unconcerned, and for fear they might betray themselves in some way to their mother and father they refrained from referring to Maria's activities at all. To Mrs. Taylor the sudden 'cessation of hostilities' was a puzzling business.

As for Mr. Taylor, he read his paper, wrote a few business letters, talked of local happenings, and smoked his pipe. Everything was quite proper; even dull. All Gregory and Pat could do was exchange grim glances and look at the clock.

It had reached eleven when Maria reappeared. She was smiling contentedly.

'Late scholar, am I not?' she asked, as

she surveyed the quartet considering her. 'After all, Mrs. Taylor, I did warn you that I had no idea when I would be returning . . . '

Mrs. Taylor smiled. 'I don't blame you one little bit for staying out on such a glorious day.'

'Well, if you will pardon me, I will retire. I had some supper at a late café in town . . . Good night.'

'Oh, Miss Black . . . ' At a meaning look from her brother Pat got quickly to her feet.

'There's — something I'd like to say to you.' Pat could feel colour flooding into her cheeks. 'It's most urgent, and — '

'Not so urgent, but what it can't wait until tomorrow, surely?' Maria responded, smiling, 'Unless, of course, it has something to do with the murder of Keith?'

Mr. Taylor peered over his reading glasses and Gregory frowned to himself. So far Maria had not stated facts in so many words or in quite such a tone.

'Well . . . ' Pat hesitated uncomfortably. 'It's very private. Maybe I ought to tell you upstairs.'

Maria shrugged. 'Oh, very well. Come along up . . . And good night again, everybody.'

Pat followed Maria's bulky form up the staircase and into the bedroom. Maria switched on the light and closed the door, laid aside her hat and sunshade.

'Now, Pat, what is it?' she asked. 'I'm very tired. I have had a most exhausting day.'

'I think that's a get-out, Miss Black,' Pat responded, her chin firming. 'You're never tired! Would it not be better to say you don't want to be bothered with me, and let it go at that?'

'Let's not waste time talking, my dear,' Maria said quietly. 'Obviously you are intending to ask me to leave, and my reply will be that I have not the least intention of doing so.'

'Good Lord!' Pat exclaimed.

Maria chuckled at the girl's blank surprise and went across to the dressing table. Seating herself, she began to unfasten her bun of hair, looking at Pat in the mirror.

'It is perfectly plain,' Maria explained, 'that my presence in this house is causing increasingly of strained relations between all of us. The end of it would be to ask me to depart — and you, knowing me best, would be selected for the unenviable task of giving me my marching orders. I admire your courage, my dear, and I'm sorry that I have to refuse.'

'But you can't refuse!' Pat objected. 'After all, this isn't your house.'

'Nor is it yours.' Maria laid hairpins in the glass brush-tray. 'This house belongs to your father, young lady, and he is the one who must ask me to go, if that is required. If he does I shall still refuse. His only course then would be to go to law about it, and I don't think he'd do that . . . ' Maria's cold eyes fixed on Pat in the mirror. 'One thing might lead to another, Pat, and I cannot imagine your father being anxious to involve himself with the law under any pretext whatever — particularly as I would feel compelled to explain why I am staying on here.'

'If it comes to that, Miss Black, why are you staying on here?'

'Because this is the house in which Keith met his death, and also because the amenities are so much pleasanter than those of an hotel. Also, because I like you. You have quite a fighting spirit of your own — but I would warn you against vicious tendencies, such as those which prompted you to want Mr. Robinson to be accused of murdering his son.'

'This isn't getting us anywhere, Miss Black,' Pat said. 'You see, I want you to — '

'I know,' Maria interrupted, raising a hand imperiously. 'You are afraid that I am going to find out something which will mean the arrest of your father, and you are doing your utmost to shield him. As his daughter, that is only to be expected. But remember this: no matter what I find out — or what I have found out already — I still do not represent the law.'

Pat sank down on the edge of the bed. 'Miss Black, you mean you know all about Dad? What he's done? Oh, my — *God!*'

'I know that he was the first in the cellar and thereby had the time in which to do many things,' Maria responded.

'And I can well understand that you and your brother are perhaps trying to get rid of me and so save the situation . . . ' Maria got to her feet and came over to put an arm about the girl's shoulders. 'Take my advice, Pat, and let things work themselves out in their own way.'

Pat got to her feet and stood wondering. Maria looked at her, then asked a question.

'Did your brother ever ask you anything about the drug administered to Keith? How long it took to have an effect?'

'No,' Pat answered dully. 'Does it matter?'

'That depends upon the point of view.'

Pat hesitated, almost said something, then thought better of it. She drifted over to the door and Maria opened it for her.

'Good night, Pat,' she said quietly, and closed the door after her.

A few minutes later she was settled in bed she set about the task of bringing her notes up to date:

I have had an interesting day, commencing with what I believe was an accurate reconstruction of the method by which the shadow of the 'dead man' was produced. Clearly this was faked — though so cleverly, that I am left with the conviction that the idea was borrowed from a plotted story somewhere. I do not think anybody in normal life could have thought of the idea from scratch.

This afternoon I tracked down the sister of Keith's mother. From what she told me I now believe that the coroner, the police, and even I myself, based everything on the wrong assumption from the very start. Namely, that Keith inherited insanity from his mother.

As I see it, her insanity was not of such a terribly serious order at the time he was born, though medical evidence at the coroner's inquest seemed to suggest that her condition was such as to produce a mentally weak child. It was, at best, the only theory since the real truth escaped everybody, myself included. I think now that I have the truth — clearly and vividly — and it is my intention to pursue it to the end.

If Gregory had not taken it upon himself to assume the blame for drugging *that wine I too would have accepted the obvious and made a big mistake. That gave me pause — time to think — and get at the root of things.*

I must see Mr. Martin first thing tomorrow and forward my plans. I might also do worse than have a watch kept on Gregory.

The time is 11.45 p.m.

★ ★ ★

Pat had just finished dressing the following morning when she called 'Come in' to an urgent rapping on the door of her room. It was Gregory who entered, a towel thrown over his shoulder.

'Well, what happened?' he demanded. 'I didn't see you again last night after you'd followed Black Maria upstairs. Did you talk to her?'

'Only for about ten minutes. Then I came on to bed. I couldn't tell you how I'd got on because Mum and Dad were down there with you, and besides . . . there was nothing to tell. She won't go and she defies Dad, Mum, you, or anybody else to make her.'

Gregory's eyes narrowed. 'Okay. Then that shifts the responsibility on to me.'

Pat caught his arm urgently as he turned to the door. 'Greg,' she pleaded, 'please don't do anything desperate! That would only make things worse than ever.'

'It just couldn't,' he retorted. 'The most desperate thing at the moment is that Dad's in danger and — '

'But I'm not so sure that he is! From what Miss Black said — '

'Just a minute,' Gregory said slowly. 'You didn't tell her about Dad, surely? About what we think?'

'It wasn't necessary. She told *me*!' Pat's voice became insistent. 'And the only reason she doesn't act is because she still isn't satisfied . . . Surely that means there may still be a chance that we're wrong about Dad?'

Gregory shook his head.

'It means only one thing to me,' he answered. 'She has got to be made to go, and stop investigating. And I'm not kidding either!' Then he was gone, closing the door sharply behind him.

Pat went down to breakfast moodily; and she was still in this frame of mind when she departed for business.

Not so Gregory. There was a hard, brittle determination about him, and his acid way of dealing with quite commonplace conversation brought more than one surprised glance from his parents. When he left the house it was on his bicycle — for a change — and he did not go to business in the normal way, either. Instead he rang up the office and invented a client upon whom he thought it might prove beneficial to call. He did not particularly care what excuse he made: he was concentrated upon only one thing — watching the activities of Maria and molding his plans for removing her.

Maria herself left the house in her Austin Seven when she had breakfasted, and drove in to town.

She did not observe Gregory in the far distance, keeping track of her, a task he did not find particularly difficult with Maria's sedate driving.

She drew up first outside the post

office and went inside the building to a telephone-box. Here Gregory was stumped, but he remained at a distance, wondering what would happen next.

In a few minutes she was speaking on the phone to Dr. Herbert Chalmers, the psychologist who taught the mysteries of the mind to erring young ladies at Roseway once a week.

'Miss Black! So glad to hear your voice!' Dr. Chalmers had a fruity bass. 'How are you? I understand from the House-mistress that you are attending to — '

'A moment, Doctor,' Maria interposed. 'My main reason for disturbing you is to ask a favour. Very shortly I am hoping to make a personal call upon you — at your home — with a letter. It will be from a friend of mine. I shall want you to read it, not for the written matter it contains but for the handwriting. In other words, use your knowledge of psychology to analyse the writing. You understand?'

'You mean character from handwriting?'

'Yes. You can do that, can you not?'

The psychologist chuckled. 'Most certainly I can. Merely routine work in my profession. Any time, Miss Black. You can rely on it.'

'Splendid, Doctor, I thought I could — but I considered it only fair to warn you in advance.'

'I — er — suppose I cannot ask why you — '

'I would take it as a great favour if you wouldn't.'

'Ah — quite! Rest assured that your confidence will be respected.'

Maria rang off, then made another call. She spoke to the hostel further down the street, secured Pulp, and told him to meet her outside the hostel in a few minutes. Then, smiling to herself, she left the post office.

Not by so much as a second's hesitation did she advertise the fact that she had caught a distant glimpse of Gregory Taylor leaning on his bicycle. He was on the opposite side of the road, some way off, considering a shop window.

'Dear me, the old trick of watching the reflection in a shop window,' Maria murmured.

She regained her car and proceeded

without haste down the main street, stopping again outside the hostel. Pulp Martin, lounging against the wall and enjoying the blaze of summer sunlight, raised an arm in greeting and came forward.

'Hiya, Maria . . . ' He peered in at her through the open window. 'Everything okay?'

'Very much okay, Mr. Martin.' Maria beamed on him and patted the seat beside her. 'Come on in — But before you do, take a careful glance round and see if you can spot a young man in a navy-blue suit with very dark shiny hair riding a bicycle. Take a note of his appearance for future reference.'

Pulp withdrew his head from the car. Whistling idly, he surveyed the scenery and finally strolled round the back of the car and sank into the seat beside Maria.

'Yeah, I seed him,' he acknowledged. 'About fifty yards down the road, a guy trying to put a chain on his bike.'

Maria chuckled. 'So *that's* the gag now, is it? Like pausing to tie your shoelace. Poor Gregory! I'm afraid his methods of

306

trying to keep me under observation are a trifle amateur.'

'You mean that young guy is followin' you? Huh, I'll dumed soon — '

'No, you won't, Mr. Martin!' Maria put a restraining hand on his arm. 'Don't even betray the fact that we know anything about it. I have the feeling that under the misguided notion that he may be helping things he may try and attack me at some time that is why from now on I want you to keep a constant watch on him . . . That is, of course, when we are not together.'

'You mean you're in danger, Maria?' Pulp asked grimly.

'I consider it is possible,' Maria admitted, sighing. 'I cannot look in every direction at once, so I am asking you to keep an eye on him.'

'You bet I will!'

'And now to business, Mr. Martin. I am going to need your assistance tonight for what may unashamedly be called a burglary.'

Pulp grinned. 'Right up my street!'

'Quite so, but I have not your enviable

gift for — hmm — thumbing my nose at law and order . . . We are going to burgle the premises of Mr. Ambrose Robinson. I want a letter, or a note — or anything at all — provided it is in Mr. Robinson's handwriting. For another thing I wish to examine the contents of his pockets.'

'Well, I guess that can be done okay,' Pulp agreed. 'Won't be the first time I've done a spot of friskin'. But look if you want some writing from this guy Robinson why don't y' just write him a letter an' get his reply?'

'You are slipping, Mr. Martin,' Maria reproved. 'Where is the guarantee that he would reply? And in any case that expedient would not permit me to search his pockets.'

'What in heck do you expect to find in his pockets?'

'I've no idea. I am simply playing one of my occasional hunches.'

'What's all this mumbo-jumbo about Robinson? I thought he was in the clear.'

'Perhaps he is: I am not yet sure. I am simply testing every angle before I make up my mind. There have been — and still are — many twists and turns in this business. It should not be long now before we are sure. If we should find some writing belonging to Mr. Robinson I am going to have it analysed by a very good friend of mine — a Dr. Chalmers. He is on the tuition staff at Roseway. He is quite a brilliant psychologist.'

'Yeah? I don't go for these guys who prod your subconscience or whatever it is — '

'*Subconscious*, Mr. Martin! However, now you know what I intend doing.'

'But that won't start until tomorrow at the earliest — and we don't case Robinson's joint until tonight. So what do we do in the meantime?'

Maria smiled. 'I think, Mr. Martin, that we should spend the day together — if only to wear out Gregory Taylor's admirable patience.'

'But ain't there sump'n *important* we can do?'

'Not until tonight. Everything else has been done. I have, as you would put it, got this case 'in the bag'.'

'That's swell hearin', Maria. All right,

where do we go? I'm allergic to lookin' in museums and stores. Wimmin is more my angle — '

'Of that I am disturbingly aware . . . This morning I think we will park the car and then walk hither and yon with the sole object of tiring Mr. Gregory Taylor. We will then have lunch, and this afternoon we might drop in at the cinema to see a film of your choice . . . '

Pulp's eyes brightened. 'Sure we will! A film with dames in it . . . Suits me fine! But say, you don't go for pin-ups, surely?'

'Presumably,' Maria said, clearing her throat primly, 'there will be a leading man in the film. Thus, Mr. Martin, we compromise and enjoy our respective — er — favourites. Hmm — quite!'

★　★　★

Maria and Pulp saw Gregory Taylor for a moment as they emerged from a side street café after lunch — selected in order that her somewhat extraordinary escort might not attract too much notice — and they saw him again when they emerged from the cinema after the matinée.

'I fancy he will not attempt anything until he knows that I am without you,' Maria commented, as they settled in the Austin.

'In that case it ain't goin' to be safe for you to go back to the Taylor joint.'

'It could hardly be safer,' Maria contradicted. 'He will not attempt anything with the rest of the family present: it is outside, if anywhere, where he will attempt something — if he can. I look to you to keep your eyes open.'

'You betcha. What do we do now, then?'

'I'll drop you at the hostel, then I shall return to the Taylor home, spend the evening there, and will meet you outside the hostel again at two o'clock in the morning . . . I take it you will be able to get out?'

'You know me,' Pulp said.

'Good! After that we will proceed to Mr. Robinson's.'

At the hostel Maria left him and in the car's rear mirror caught a distant view of Gregory Taylor fiddling with his bicycle at the kerb.

311

She drove on up the main street and out to the environs where the Taylor home lay. At length she reached Cypress Avenue, drove the car into the driveway, and was admitted into the house by Mrs. Taylor.

'Been touring round?' Mrs. Taylor asked, as she closed the front door.

'I have been seeing the sights,' Maria responded dryly. 'And some very unusual sights, too.' She turned to the staircase, then Mrs. Taylor gave her pause.

'I'd like to know something, Miss Black. Have you given up the matter of Keith? You seem to be able to spend your time touring round the sights of Redford, which makes me think that — '

'You are falling into the habit of jumping to conclusions,' Maria reproved, and she smiled disarmingly. 'Quite a dangerous habit . . . ' And she went on up the stairs to her room before the subject could develop.

When she came downstairs again she found Gregory and his father both seated in the front room, awaiting their evening meal. Maria could not help but smile inwardly as she noticed Gregory's sullen face and the considerable sunburning he had acquired.

When Pat arrived the meal commenced, and as usual Maria did full justice to her share. She only spoke when spoken to and deliberately evaded any questions that hovered near the problem of Keith's murder. Then at length she delivered a surprise.

'I think,' she said, 'I shall be leaving within the next day or two — and somehow I have the feeling that none of you will try and prevail upon me to stay.'

'Seems to me,' Gregory said, his pale eyes on her, 'that only two reasons could make you go. Either you have decided to give up this business as a bad job and let the edict of the law stand; or else you know how the murder was committed, and by whom.'

'The latter,' Maria said, 'is the case. But more than that I prefer not to say at this stage.'

'Then I think you should!' Mrs. Taylor declared, with unusual sharpness. 'You spend your time sightseeing — and now you say you have the problem solved! Why don't you do something, then? Can't you see that our nerves — '

'I am waiting,' Maria said, 'for proof.'

Mr. Taylor stirred, looked up from his meal. 'Did someone say sightseeing?' he asked vaguely. 'Where?'

'I imagine,' Maria answered, with a grim look towards Gregory, 'that your son might be able to give an even clearer account of my movements than I can myself.'

'Greg can? But — ?'

'You are not very experienced in the art of shadowing, young man,' Maria commented. 'Your only virtue in that direction is your untiring patience.'

'All right, so you saw me!' Gregory said bitterly. 'I don't care if you did! I thought I ought to keep my eye on you because of the suspicion you seem to have against all of us. I've no idea what you're aiming at, but I am prepared to fight to the last ditch for my mother, father, and sister. So I'm watching everything you do — and if you try anything tough I don't care what lengths I go to try and stop you!'

Something seemed to occur to Mrs. Taylor. 'So that's why you didn't come home to lunch!'

'I strongly disapprove of such behaviour!' Mr. Taylor snapped. 'I am quite sure Miss Black knows what she is doing — and besides, what about the office?'

'The office can wait. I've other things on my mind.'

Maria, having precipitated action, sat back and watched it develop. Mr. Taylor was, for once, shaken out of his geniality into real anger.

'What exactly do you imagine Miss Black is going to do which makes it necessary for you to shadow her?' he demanded. 'I never heard of such confounded impudence towards a guest. Explain yourself!'

'It's just one of Greg's crazy ideas, Dad,' Pat interjected. You know how it is. He's read so many detective stories in his time that he thinks — '

'Just a minute, sis!' Gregory's voice was icy. 'I'm not going to sit here and be slanged when I'm only trying to help,' he went on. 'In fact I don't see any reason why things should be kept wrapped up any longer. I'm doing everything I can, Dad, to protect you!'

'And what am I supposed to have done?'

Gregory gave him a baffled look. 'Miss Black knows what you've done; Pat knows; I know — and you know! About Keith . . . It — it just couldn't have been anybody else but you, Dad.'

'Are you daring to accuse me of having murdered him?' Mr. Taylor nearly shouted.

'Everything fits in,' Gregory retorted. 'You drugged the wine, for which I took the blame — to try and make things easier for you, chiefly because I felt I'd be better able to deal with Miss Black than you.'

'I drugged the wine?' Mr. Taylor repeated blankly. 'Where did you get that idea?'

'It could only have been you. I worked it all out.'

'Then you'd better stop riding the wrong horse!' Mr. Taylor did not look annoyed any longer. He seemed to be struggling with an immense surprise.

'Oh, this is impossible!' Gregory cried. 'It had to be you who dealt with Keith, because you were the first in the cellar. The way this business works out — as Miss Black will verify — it is perfectly clear that whoever went into the cellar first after Keith's shadow being seen — must be the murderer.'

'Well, I'm not responsible,' Mr. Taylor insisted, 'and the sooner you stop thinking such crack-brained things the better.'

Gregory opened his mouth to speak and then closed it again. Pat's bewildered gaze went from him to her father — then to Maria. Maria's face was completely expressionless.

'What do you think, Miss Black?' Mrs. Taylor asked anxiously.

'I think,' Maria said, 'that the less said the better.'

It was perfectly clear that all four would have liked to say a good deal, but she maintained a rigid silence and refused to answer questions. Finally the quartet gave up the effort and drifted into their routine activities for the evening.

Maria kept a little apart in a corner, apparently absorbed in a back number of a weekly magazine, but mentally she was taking to pieces everything that had been said during the evening meal . . .

14

It was 10.30 when Maria retired and she did not spend any time making up her notes. There was work to be done during the night, and if it was to be done properly sleep now was the essential thing.

She instructed herself to awaken at 1.15, and did so to the minute to find the house deadly quiet. Silently, without bothering to switch on the light, since she had all her clothes in readiness, she dressed, finally adding a warm topcoat and a beret. Then, with her torch in one pocket and a bundle of keys in the other, she glided out of the bedroom, stepped over the loose board on the landing, and crept downstairs.

She left the house by means of the front window, pulling the curtains back into position across it when she was outside. Any chance visit downstairs by any member of the family would reveal the front door still bolted — and it was unlikely that the windows would be examined with the curtains covering them . . .

Refreshed and active despite the brevity of her sleep, she strode on down the quiet road in the still summer night air, pausing every now and again to look and listen. There was no sign of anybody following.

Having timed herself perfectly, Maria entered the high street of Redford at five minutes to two by the General Market clock tower. It was chiming two as she turned the corner to the hostel — and immediately a figure loomed out of the shadows.

Pulp Martin came forward swiftly. 'All set, Maria?'

'Yes, Mr. Martin. Come.'

He fell into step beside her and they went up the road in the direction of Ambrose Robinson's shop. Pulp glanced behind him once or twice as he walked.

'What about that guy Greg Taylor?' he asked presently.

'I don't think he followed me,' Maria replied. 'He had no idea I intended to make an early morning jaunt in this fashion, and I am sure he would not stay awake all night to see if I did . . . Ah, that is Robinson's shop,' she broke off, as they turned a corner. 'The fourth one along. See it?'

Pulp looked intently. A street lamp was glowing about ten yards away from the shop.

'Looks like a natural to me,' Pulp murmured, 'but I'm scared of cops on the prowl. Is there a back way in? Always safer, I reckon.'

'That I don't know — but there is a back yard. I remember seeing it from the window of the room where I talked to Mr. Robinson.'

'That's all we need, Maria. Let's take a gander.'

Maria followed Pulp and discovered he was counting the number of shops from the entry to Ambrose Robinson's premises. They went down the entry together and Pulp began counting again, pausing finally at a high yard door dimly visible in the starlight.

'Okay, this is it,' he whispered. 'I'll get

over and then I'll let you in.'

He muscled himself up gently to the top of the door, slid over it and dropped to the other side into a small enclosure of yard. His running pumps made no sound whatever. In a matter of seconds he had admitted Maria and they glided to the nearest window. It proved to be too tough a proposition, so Pulp turned his attention to the pantry.

Here everything was in his favour. The hot weather was no doubt the reason for the window being slightly open at the top. Pulp opened it to the limit, and by dint of squirming and wriggling he managed to ease himself silently inside.

There was an interval, then Maria saw the back door open. She glided silently into a kitchen and there was the sound of Pulp shutting the door. The little oblong of starlight vanished and the blackness was complete.

'Now what?' he whispered.

'We'd better make sure that Mr. Robinson is asleep first,' she breathed. 'Lead on upstairs.'

She pulled out her torch, masked the

beam with her fingers, and together they moved soundlessly along the narrow hall and up the even narrower staircase. An open doorway, from beyond which came the sound of deep breathing, was sufficient to guide them.

'He's right out,' Pulp breathed, then he muttered something as the pocket of his jacket caught the doorknob and rattled it.

The man beyond coughed and sniffed once or twice — there was a long, anguishing silence — then Ambrose Robinson began breathing deeply again.

'Hell's sweet little bells,' Pulp muttered. 'That sure gave me the sweats, Maria.'

'Don't you know a trick for putting people to sleep if they get fractious?' Maria whispered. 'Something harmless? Pressure on the arteries? I seem to remember you used such a method once.'

'Yeah, I sure do. Want me to try it?'

'Only if Mr. Robinson should awaken. Stand by him and be ready. I wish to search his suit . . . '

Pulp moved to the bedside and remained there with his powerful hands spread ready for instant action upon the sleeping man. Robinson was dimly visible as Maria's masked torch cast a faint reflection. He was lying on his side, his back to Pulp, and seemed to be sleeping heavily.

It was not long before Maria evidently found that for which she was looking. From Ambrose Robinson's waistcoat, thrown carelessly over a chair-back, she extracted something that looked like a small pair of folding pliers with sharply pointed jaws. Maria slipped them back in the pocket after examining them and glided to Pulp once more.

'Let's go,' she murmured — and they went downstairs.

'Find what you wanted?' Pulp whispered, as they reached the only living room in the poky little place.

'My hunch, I'm glad to say, was correct. I found a small pair of pliers with folding handles, like pocket nail scissors.'

'What the blazes have they got to do with the business?'

'It's rather a long story, Mr. Martin, and I'll have to tell it you later . . . Now,

324

help me look for a specimen of Mr. Robinson's handwriting.'

'How'll we know if it's his and not his son's writing?'

'I once saw a letter Keith wrote. It is unlikely that anybody else's writing outside Mr. Robinson's or Keith's will be here — so let me see whatever you find.'

Together they began searching drawers and cupboards, most of which were unlocked, and those that were not Maria dealt with, with the skeleton key she had on the bunch she had brought with her. It was Pulp who finally came upon something pushed inside the massive Holy Bible.

'Say, get a load of this!' he breathed. 'It sounds kinda screwy to me: 'And he said Open the window eastward. And he opened it. Then Elisha said Shoot! And he shot'. Say, Maria, who's this Elisha guy? A film prodoocer?'

'Elisha was a prophet, Mr. Martin, and though you are not aware of it you are being slightly blasphemous. I think that statement comes from the Second Kings, if I remember rightly.'

'No kiddin'? There may be some more of the stuff. This Bible's loaded up with 'em — '

'Never mind: this will do admirably, and its loss will not be noticed, I imagine. Since it isn't Keith's handwriting I hope it is Mr. Robinson's. Since it is a Biblical quotation it is highly likely . . . Now let us go,' Maria urged. 'I feel most uneasy on somebody else's premises.'

Pulp let her out at the back door, bolted it, and then got out of the house the way he had come, leaving the pantry window in its earlier position. In the same fashion he locked the yard gate after letting Maria out into the entry. Then he climbed the wall and dropped beside her. Satisfied, they moved into the shadowy dark.

But up in his bedroom Ambrose Robinson was not asleep. Nor had he been since the moment Pulp's jacket had caught on the doorknob. Through almost closed eyes, whilst he had simulated sleep, Ambrose Robinson had seen everything Maria had done in the bedroom. It had been quite enough for him without his needing to find out what had transpired downstairs.

Ambrose Robinson smiled bitterly, sighed, and gave himself up to staring absently into the dark. Fifteen minutes later he came to a decision. He got up, drew on his dressing gown, and went downstairs. Switching on the living room light, he took a sheet of blank paper from a drawer, together with an envelope. Then he sat down at the table and began to write . . .

* * *

Pulp insisted on escorting Maria back as far as the Taylor house, or at least, when she insisted, as far as the avenue in which the house stood.

'There may be somebody on the watch,' she explained. 'I can alibi myself by saying I went out for a walk, though I shall be hard put to it to explain why I used the front room window . . . But I shall certainly never be able to explain you away as well.'

'You don't want 'em to know what

you're doin', Maria? Why? I don't get it.'

'It is easily answered, Mr. Martin. I don't like any suspect to know what I am doing . . . However, as far as we are concerned the actual hard work is done. The problem is solved.'

'It is? Then mebby you'll let me in on it sometime? I ain't got the vaguest idea what's been cookin'. Who did what, and why?'

'You know me, Mr. Martin . . . all the details when the final bolt has been shot. After breakfast I shall be journeying back to Langhorn — or at least to Bollington, which is a couple of miles further — to see Dr. Chalmers with reference to this Biblical statement and get his reactions. I should be back here again by evening, at which time I shall have something to say to the Taylor family. There is no reason why you should not be present,' Maria added. 'Yes . . . be at the Taylor house at seven tomorrow evening. Or rather seven *this* evening.'

'Okay, you got a date. And what about Greg Taylor? Do I still keep my lamps on him?'

'I hardly think he would be such a fool as to try trailing me again after my exposing his activities to him. Still, if you wish.'

'I will!' Pulp decided grimly. 'I ain't takin' no chances where you're concerned, Maria. You mean more to me than a mother.'

'I do? Well now, I feel most gratified . . . Good night, Mr. Martin.'

' 'Night, Maria.'

Maria returned into the Taylor home by the way she had left it to find everything still quiet. Only when she reached the safety of her bedroom, without mishap, did she heave a sigh of relief. She put Ambrose Robinson's Biblical note safely away in her suitcase, undressed, and then climbed thankfully into bed. She debated whether or not she ought to enter up her final conclusions in her record book, and then found that she must have fallen asleep in the act of making up her mind.

There was brilliant sunlight in the room and the sound of crockery being washed in the domestic regions. Surprised, she saw that it was half past nine.

'Preposterous!' she snorted, furious with herself. 'Take something away from Nature and she'll take it back — even sleep. I had hoped to be on my way by this time.'

She dressed and washed hurriedly, arriving downstairs to find Mrs. Taylor in the midst of washing up. She brought in the breakfast that she had been keeping warm.

'Late this morning, Miss Black,' she commented.

'Yes, indeed. My peregrinations in the fresh air yesterday, I think. And I greatly appreciate your keeping the breakfast ready for me.'

'And why shouldn't I? You're our guest, are you not?'

Maria smiled faintly. 'By this time, Mrs. Taylor, I think you are alone in that opinion. I am afraid that the rest of the family look upon me in the same light as prisoners look upon the governor of the jail.'

'Oh, well, we don't all think alike, thank goodness.' Mrs. Taylor observed, philosophically.

Maria went on with her meal for a moment and then motioned for Mrs. Taylor to sit down. She did so and joined Maria in a cup of tea.

'I shall be leaving tomorrow, Mrs. Taylor,' Maria announced. 'I'm sure you'll be glad to know that.'

'I'm not even thinking about that.' Mrs. Taylor said. 'I'm wondering what you are going to do or say before you leave. You remember your promise to me . . . that if you found out anything about my family you would let me know beforehand?'

'I remember,' Maria assented quietly. 'There are quite a few things I shall want to explain this evening, not only to you but to all of you. That is if your husband, Pat, and Gregory will be home at the usual time?'

'As far as I know they will, yes.'

'Splendid!' Maria hurried through the remainder of her breakfast and then got to her feet. 'Now I really must be going. I have a most urgent call to make — and I shall not be back before evening.'

In ten minutes she was on her way in the Austin Seven, headed in the direction of Bollinton, a journey of fifty miles.

She stopped only once — at a drive-in for a cup of her beloved tea; then she went on again to arrive in familiar Bollington, close to Langhorn and Roseway College, at half past twelve. Here she lunched and then drove on to Professor Chalmers' home on the outskirts of the town.

She was with him for a couple of hours, then with a grimly determined face she commenced the return journey.

At the same drive-in she stopped for another cup of tea, then once more was on her way. She was humming contentedly to herself and had nearly reached Redford when she became aware of the furious blaring of a horn behind her. She looked in the rear mirror and saw a radiator close upon her.

Drawing in to the side, she undulated her right hand in serpentine motions for the car to follow through; instead there was a sudden thundering concussion and a violent jolt. The steering wheel was whipped out of her grasp and she was flung across it. Her head struck the windscreen with savage violence and the universe seemed to explode in blue lights and tumultuous roaring.

When she opened her eyes again she was looking into a red face crowned with upstanding carroty hair. As background for the head there was cobalt-blue sky.

'Gosh, Maria, I'm glad t'see you movin' again,' Pulp breathed. 'I thought that lowdown skunk had got you for sure . . .'

Maria stirred painfully and rubbed a swelling bruise on her forehead. She felt dizzy as she sat up. She found she was lying on the grassy bank at the side of the long, deserted road. Her Austin was half tipped on its side into the ditch.

'What in the world happened?' she demanded blankly.

'Happened! It were that guy Greg Taylor! He did his best to kill you . . . and muffed it. How are you feelin'? Shall I run to a 'phone or get an ambulance, or somethin'?'

'Good gracious, no, Mr. Martin. My head aches and I seem to have a wonderful bruise, but otherwise — Dear me!' Maria looked astonished for a moment. 'I must have been stunned. But . . . how do you come to be here so providentially?'

'Nothing much to it,' Pulp answered. 'Even though you said it wasn't no longer important, I kept my lamps on that Greg Taylor guy just the same. I was around this morning when you left the Taylor place in your Austin. I figured that if I watched you, that wus all that mattered. I didn't need to watch Taylor so long as you wus safe. Well, Gregory Taylor watched you leave. I saw him, see. He was at the end of the avenoo in a car — pretty old-fashioned one judgin' from the boot — or rumble-seat as you call 'em in this half-pint country.'

'He must have borrowed it from somebody,' Maria said. 'The Taylor car is broken down at the moment . . . but go on. What did you do?'

'I took a chance. From where I was I could see him watchin' which way you wus goin': I figured he was set on followin' you. I stopped him, though!' Pulp grinned hugely. 'Before he could start his motor I slipped up behind the car and stuck my handkerchief in the end of the exhaust pipe. Naturally the engine wouldn't fire. Boy, was he burned up! He nearly wrecked his starter!

'I kept out of sight at the back of the car. He got out to monkey around with the engine, then I figured that mebby I'd better see what he was aimin' at, so I took my hanky back and climbed in the rumble-seat, pulling the lid down after me. He didn't see me: his head was shoved inside the engine. If he'd have looked in the rumble-seat for tools or sump'n I was all set t'hit him so hard he'd have hit Jupiter.

'He didn't, though. He got the jollopy goin' only he didn't go far. Lost you, I guess. I found we'd stopped at a corner a bit lower down the road here. I remained where I was — and heck! I sure got the cramp. He just sat . . . and sat . . . waitin'.'

'To see if I came back,' Maria said in a grim voice. 'He must have driven through the town and noticed that my car was nowhere to be seen. He knows this is the only road into town and from that corner there he could see all this main road, whereas I wouldn't notice him. Then when at last he recognized my car he tried to run me down.'

'That's it,' Pulp agreed. 'The jolt when he hit you fair knocked my teeth out. I lifted the lid to see what had happened and why we'd stopped. I saw your Austin had been knocked fer a loop. I risked gettin' out. I guess he didn't see me: he wus too busy lookin' ahead and getting' away.'

Maria got unsteadily to her feet.

'Apparently that young man is most determined to get me out of the way,' she commented. 'I'm more than glad you were keeping watch, Mr. Martin. Remind me to recompense you . . . Now I think you had better find a garage and have them get my car back on the road.'

'Garage nothin',' Pulp said in contempt, and took off his jacket.

Maria stood and watched as he bared his muscular arms, then going over to the car he seized it below the radiator and heaved with all his strength. Concentrated effort lifted the front portion back on to the road. Pulp waited a moment or two and then did a similar feat with the back.

'Amazing!' Maria declared, walking over to him.

'I guess this jollopy's taken a shellacking,' Pulp observed, pointing to a dented wing, a twisted bumper, and a smashed headlamp. The cellulose, too, had been badly scraped.

'These troubles can be taken care of with the insurance,' Maria said. 'It is the deliberate effort made by Gregory to try and kill me with which I'm concerned.'

'Yeah,' Pulp gave a grim nod. 'What do you figure on doin' about it?'

Maria fingered the bruise on her forehead. 'As far as I can see there is nothing I can do,' she sighed. 'Complaining to the police would not do any good. I think it will have to be classed as an unsuccessful effort to eliminate me, and let it go at that. At the moment I have too many other things on my mind to be bothered with the matter.'

'You have, huh?' Pulp's voice sounded

as though he were thinking of something else.

'I'm bringing this business to an end the moment I get back to the Taylor home,' Maria added.

'Which is what Gregory Taylor hopes will never happen, I guess. Okay . . . let's see if the motor works.'

The engine started up first time. Pulp held the door open for Maria to sit at the steering wheel. As he settled beside her he gave her a glance.

'You said I could come and hear what you've got to say to the Taylors, Maria. That okay?'

'Perfectly,' Maria assented, beginning to recover rapidly from her misadventure.

During the remainder of the trip to Cypress Avenue Pulp did not say anything — which for him was quite unusual. He still said nothing when they had reached the Taylor home. He opened the car door for Maria and helped her alight; then he stood beside her as she rang the front doorbell.

It was Pat who opened the door. The moment she did so all the passiveness went from Pulp. In one mighty bound he leapt forward, whirled the astonished Pat to one side, and charged into the front room.

Mr. and Mrs. Taylor were there, just preparing to settle at the laid table. Gregory Taylor was by the window, staring out worriedly upon the Austin Seven. He glanced round and then staggered backwards with an agonized grunt as an iron fist smote him under the jaw.

'Some things I'll stand for, feller . . . some things I won't,' Pulp breathed, his face crimson with fury and excitement. 'No cheap two-cent shyster lawyer is goin' to push Maria around if I know it . . . Get on your feet, blast you!'

Gregory remained motionless, his pale eyes startled. He had fallen against the back of the chesterfield. He darted a quick glance about him for the nearest way of escape.

Pulp lunged, seized Gregory by the coat collar and dragged him across the chesterfield. A left pistoned and slammed into Gregory's stomach. He doubled up.

He jerked straight again as a right-hander again took him on the jaw. Helplessly he sailed into the laid table and crashed half across it.

'Mr. Martin! Mr. *Martin*!' Maria shouted, coming into the room. '*Stop it!*'

'Not on your life, Maria,' Pulp retorted. 'This monkeyin' around fer a legal angle has gone on long enough. When this guy starts tryin' to rub you out it's time to take the gloves off . . . '

The others did not say anything; they were too utterly astounded. Pulp dived forward before Gregory could completely fall off the table. He pinned him down with one hand. With the other he whipped up a tumbler from the table and smashed the top away sharply against the table edge.

Then he lowered the vicious, jagged edges until they were within a couple of inches of Gregory's sweating, terrified face.

'Okay, feller, spill it!' Pulp commanded.

Maria came and seized his shoulder but he shook her away.

'Talk, blast you!' Pulp yelled.

Moisture rolled down Gregory's pasty face. 'All right — I did it,' he panted. 'I — I tried to run Miss Black down — '

'We know that, you dope! What else do you know?'

'I don't know anything!'

'Don't hand me that! Who killed that guy Keith? Was it you?'

'No — no!' Gregory shouted. 'Honest to God it wasn't! It was Dad! He arranged everything!'

'I don't believe it — '

Pulp lowered the jagged glass slightly, then he stopped as something prodded his side. He glanced up. Mr. Taylor was standing beside him, his round face coldly menacing. In his hand was the long, sharply pointed bread saw.

15

'Let the boy alone,' Mr. Taylor ordered. 'If you don't — !' He jabbed the bread saw gently. 'He's speaking the truth — '

'He *is*?' Pulp straightened up and pushed the tumbled red hair from his face. He tossed the smashed glass down on the table. 'Okay, that settles it. Now we're getting some place.'

He glanced at Maria. 'Nothing like a bit of fist to knock sense into a guy, Maria. Beats your kid-glove technique.'

Maria's face was grim. 'I wish you would learn to control your temper, Mr. Martin! You have completely precipitated things. However, I realize that you did most of it on my behalf. I suppose my having been nearly murdered does call for some kind of retaliation.'

'You — nearly murdered?' Pat cried in horror. 'Who — '

'Me!' Gregory snarled, getting up and nursing his jaw. 'I tried to finish this old snooper by running her into a ditch. It looks as though I miscalculated — '

'Did you do it to save me from being arrested?' Mr. Taylor demanded, throwing down the bread saw.

'Yes! And I might as well have saved myself the trouble. Now you've gone and admitted everything.'

Mr. Taylor shook his head. 'No I haven't. I simply said that you were speaking the truth when you said that I arranged everything. I *did* — and to put an end to this confounded business I might as well admit it — but I did not kill Keith.'

Silence. Maria cleared her throat, and then motioned to chairs. Each one of them slowly sat down.

'You, Mr. Taylor,' she said, 'have admitted something that I already knew . . . that you arranged everything but were prevented from killing Keith . . . You did intend to kill him, didn't you?'

'Yes, I did.'

Maria nodded slowly. 'You intended to kill him from the moment you knew he was engaged to Pat, and the idea of killing him if he became engaged to her had, I think, been conceived quite a time before. Your reason for doing it was because you had long suspected that Keith was mentally unsound. You verified this conclusion, I suggest, by getting information from the Sunbeam Home of Rest, which institution Mr. Robinson had mentioned once in conversation.'

'Right,' Taylor admitted. 'I'd guessed for a long time that Keith was queer somewhere. I fully intended to kill him if he dared to marry Pat. There was no other way to break their affinity for each other. She was infatuated with him. The evening she came home and announced that she and Keith were engaged I put a preconceived plan in motion. The first thing I did was drug his wine. Later, when I asked Pat how long a time had elapsed before Keith had collapsed I knew roughly how long this drug took to act on him.'

'All of which I had assumed,' Maria said. 'I know what you did in the cellar, and I think the scheme was worked out well in advance from a story or idea you may have read somewhere. I cannot believe that you were so original of your own volition.'

'It was based on a story called *The Hanging Shadow* in one of Greg's magazines,' Mr. Taylor replied. 'The circumstances happened to fit perfectly. Once I had made up my mind to commit a perfect crime I learned all I could about the *mistakes* criminals have made in the past. It seemed to me that the biggest one was to appear too interested in the crime . . . So I endeavoured to seem as unconcerned as possible, even after I had made the staggering discovery that the job had been done for me! I was astounded and then relieved. It meant that I really *could* appear unconcerned because I was not guilty. I'd arranged it, but not performed it.'

'Quite,' Maria assented, 'which is why you denied all your son's accusations yesterday when he said that you had done it. I too fell into the same trap. I reasoned everything out, even to several small facts — such as, only a fairly strong, tall man could have heaved Keith up to the beam.

I also wondered if a man of your dimensions could get in the chimney to fix the nail, but Mr. Martin assured me this was possible . . . Then I became puzzled. Gregory and you seemed equally guilty — he because he had admitted drugging the wine, and you because you had obviously arranged everything. I did not know at that time that Gregory was covering up.'

'His admission gave me a surprise too,' Mr. Taylor said, glancing at Gregory as he sat suddenly in a corner. 'I never expected Gregory would piece so much together. I admit I felt perturbed when I knew Pat was going to ask you here, Miss Black, because I had heard of your criminological activities, Then I decided to risk it . . . Well, since Gregory seemed determined to protect me, and I had not really done anything, I thought it safest to let things work out. I even wondered at times if Gregory hadn't done it!'

'Thanks,' Gregory said sourly.

'The possibility of the blame being divided equally over both of you gave me time to think,' Maria said. 'Then I recalled certain other factors . . . When Keith vanished Pat went to look for him and failed to find him — then his father went to look for him too. His father! What about *him*? Long ago it had been suggested to me by Pat that a locksmith, that Mr. Robinson is, might have had something to do with it, and I pooh-poohed the idea. Then I realized that perhaps I had been hasty. As near as I could tell there had been almost fifteen minutes in which Mr. Robinson had been absent from the party. I decided to look further . . . '

Maria meditated for a space fingering her watch-chain.

'The whole crux of the problem was the locked door,' she resumed. 'The key was turned, on the inside. Why look for a difficult answer? Why not the *obvious* technique of a locksmith? Namely — to turn the key with narrow-jawed pliers from the outside, the pliers gripping the end of the key? I examined the key and found scratches that could be accounted for by the action of plier jaws. It later occurred to me that having pliers at the exact moment was more than a coincidence. Was it not possible that a locksmith might carry a small pair about with him, as the clerk carries his pen, and the jeweller his lens? I — er — investigated in Mr. Robinson's home and found folding pliers in his waistcoat pocket. Evidently they are part of his 'daily equipment', so to speak.'

'Then it was Ambrose who killed Keith?' Taylor asked.

'There's no doubt of it. What I am wondering is: what made Keith go and lock himself in the cellar in the first place? Since you planned everything, Mr. Taylor, only you can answer that.'

'It is simple enough. I drugged his lemonade, timed it, and when I knew it should soon be taking effect I said to him: 'There's a present waiting for you in the cellar which I wish you'd give to Pat during the party — as coming from you. It's something she really wants, and I know she'll love it. Lock the cellar door, though, in case she follows you'. He fell for it because on the first occasion when I had taken him down in the cellar with me

348

— to provide the necessary 'look round' which would be questioned at the inquest — I told him I was planning a surprise.'

'Ah!' Maria's eyes gleamed. 'Very well planned.'

'My idea,' Taylor went on, 'was that when he had locked himself in he would collapse, roll out of sight at the bottom of the curving stairs, and the rest was up to me. Only it wasn't! When I got down there he was hanging. It was not the cardboard shadow I had arranged. That had been taken away, but not the lamp in the chimney. If anybody was mystified, that person was me. I then assumed the only possible answer — that Keith had killed himself.'

Maria's eyes moved to Pat. 'You said the shadow was not clear cut, but hazy round the edges. A hanging body would not have been hazy round the edges.'

'I only said as far as I could remember,' Pat pointed out. 'I couldn't really be sure.'

'No; I was aware of that — but fortunately your remark led me to the theory of a cutout, which would have been used had not the body itself taken its place.' Maria reflected, then looked at Mr. Taylor again. 'Tell me, Mr. Taylor, about the wine you drugged. You had the drug on your person, I take it?'

'I had. I'd carried tablets round with me for long enough, intending to use them in a celebration drink if Keith ever decided to get engaged to Pat. That was easy, since *I* called for drinks.'

'I see.' Maria's eyes moved to Gregory. 'Mr. Taylor, you referred — when first hinting at the fact that you believed Keith had been murdered — to a mortgage he was intending to take out. Was that true?'

'It was a gag,' Gregory growled. 'All part of my idea to try and outsmart you, Miss Black. I deliberately built up every angle to give a convincing reason for my believing in Keith's murder — without involving my father, of course.'

'You say Ambrose Robinson did it, Miss Black?' Mrs. Taylor asked. 'Why should he want to murder his own son?'

'Ambrose Robinson,' Maria replied quietly, 'is a criminal lunatic, who conceivably reached that condition through a violent form of religious mania. In its most virulent state, religious mania, so the psychologists tell us, is a cover-up for sadism. I tracked down Keith's aunt and from her found out that it was Robinson's brutality that finally broke his wife's mind and landed her in an asylum to die. I also found that his cruelty had become intensified after Keith's birth. Why? I made a guess. In the son I believe he saw the reflection of himself and his own unbalanced ways. For that reason he hated his son bitterly. That father and son hated each other was no secret, but few, I think, knew how deep the cleavage went . . .

'In a word, Keith did not inherit insanity from his mother, but from his *father*, and by a queer twist of circumstances the mother was locked up and died, and the father, prating Scripture, survived. I made a point of getting some of his handwriting — always the infallible guide — and submitted it to an expert. There is no doubt at all but what the writing reveals profound mental instability.'

'What I want to know is: how did

Ambrose kill Keith?' Mr. Taylor demanded.

'Of that I am none too sure,' Maria responded. 'You, Pat, when you went to search for Keith, did not go into the cellar, I presume?'

'No. The idea never even occurred to me.'

'So you didn't see the light under the cellar door, which must certainly have been there at that time?'

Mr. Taylor looked startled. 'Mmm, I forgot that. You saw the light under the door, though, didn't you, Greg?'

Gregory nodded. Pat gave a shrug. 'Just happened that I didn't see it, that's all. Simply made things safer for you, Dad. Just the same as it helped you when I decided to go home with Keith on the evening we became engaged. You had first-hand information then of how long it had taken the drug to act: otherwise you'd have had to find out by other means.'

'I was going to make tacit enquiry from Ambrose, as a matter of fact, but you saved me the trouble.'

'I felt sure you had a strong connection

with the whole thing, Mr. Taylor, *and* that you had drugged the wine,' Maria said, 'when Pat told me that Gregory had not asked her about Keith's collapse. Had he been responsible for the drug, as he claimed, he *would* have asked — definitely . . . However, to get back to Mr. Robinson. I believe he must have seen the light under the cellar door and, having searched everywhere else knew that was the only place Keith could be. We can assume, though we don't know, that he unlocked the door with pliers when he found he could get no answer . . .

'Down in the cellar he probably found Keith, unconscious from the drug. He must have also seen the hanging shadow cast by the cardboard and from it guessed what was intended. The rope and stool were handy for him, and he is quite tall and powerful enough to have lifted his son to his death. Robinson saw that somebody was planning a perfect murder and resolved to make use of the idea himself.'

'That being so,' Mr. Taylor said, 'why didn't he let me do the job?'

'I can think of only one reason — to make sure. Everything was to hand, such a chance to be rid of his son might never occur again. He could escape all blame, and so he acted. A mentally deranged person possesses wits of extraordinary sharpness, particularly so when they are directed to a sadistic enterprise — as was the case this time. That, I think, was the reason for Mr. Robinson's weighing up the situation so rapidly . . .

'The whole business would not take him above a few minutes. Then he came back upstairs, left the light on in the cellar, and locked the door by turning the key with his pliers once again. He knew you were all talking in the front room so there was little chance of his being interrupted.'

Maria got to her feet and fingered the throbbing bruise on her forehead.

'I had a further reason for suspecting that Keith was murdered. You see, he did not die in a manner consistent with suicides. Like the police surgeon in the coroner's court, I, too, have studied Gross's *Criminal Investigation*, and in his chapter on 'Hangings and Strangulation' he says that it is the invariable habit of a suicide, and especially if the suicide be mentally unbalanced, to choose a comfortable means of committing suicide — that is to say, selecting a shawl, a cloth, a soft thick rope, or, if there is not the time to find such things, then something to hand like a pair of braces. In a word, a lunatic invariably hangs himself so that the material contacting his skin will not hurt in any way . . . In the case of Keith his neck was severely chafed by the coarse rope that had been used. I was convinced that a genuine suicide would not hurt himself to that extent.'

'From 'the psychological angle,' Gregory Taylor said, brooding, 'that's dead right. I wonder why *I* didn't think of it?'

'Of the real truth,' Maria said, after a pause, 'we can only be sure after seeing Mr. Robinson himself. I think we might all go over and see him after tea and . . . '

She paused, looking at the mantelshelf. An envelope was perched on it, addressed to *Mr. Taylor Senior*, and marked '*Personal*'.

'Extraordinary!' Maria exclaimed. 'That is Mr. Robinson's handwriting! How well I know it . . .'

'Oh yes!' Mrs. Taylor suddenly seemed to emerge from a daze. 'The letter was pushed through the door this morning, Harry, for you. When I saw it on the mat I looked outside but the person who had delivered it had gone. Such a lot of things happened when you'd come in I forgot all about it.'

'For me? Coming from Ambrose at this time?' Mr. Taylor took the letter and tore the envelope quickly. 'It may have a special significance.'

He unfolded the letter and read it. His expression gradually changed and finished in one of grimness. He handed the letter to Maria.

'How right you have been,' he said quietly. 'Read it aloud Miss Black.'

'Dear Harry,

'Before long that woman Miss Black will come to the conclusion that I murdered Keith — and she will be correct! I didn't know she was a detective

356

until after I had committed the crime. I have never been comfortable since I knew of her activities. Last night, with her American friend, she paid me a visit. I knew when she found a pair of pliers in my waistcoat pocket — which seemed to be the only thing she was looking for — that she had pieced everything together and that the game was up . . .

'I am not delivering this letter because it will clear you of suspicion (which it will) but to tell you that I do not for a moment regret having murdered Keith. I hated him! He was his mother all over again. Yes, I hated him more than I hated her! She, who never believed in my efforts to guide her into spiritual paradise, has paid for her sin — but she left Keith. He too would not heed my words when I tried to guide him. So he too has gone — as he should.

'I did my utmost to guide him aright. When he would not listen and preferred to marry your daughter I became desperate. I had even planned a way to destroy him because I knew that marriage would mean more children who, in turn,

357

would become wayward like Keith and mock me. Then, so wonderful are the ways of Providence, I found a way had been shown for me by which Keith could be removed from the temptations of this heartless world.

'In the course of looking for him on the evening of the engagement celebration I noticed, after a futile search, that there was a dim gleam of light under the cellar door. It seemed that the only possible place where Keith could have gone was the cellar. Knowing the house so well, I knew it was the cellar door, of course. It was locked and I received no answer to my knocking . . . '

Maria paused and looked round on the faces of her hearers. 'There we have our verification,' she said. 'To continue:

'A glance assured me that a key was turned in the lock on the inside. I turned it with my pocket pliers and went down into the cellar. Keith lay there unconscious. On the wall, cast by a cut-out silhouette, was the shadow of a hanging man. A few moments of reasoning convinced me that somebody in your family was as anxious as I to be rid of Keith. But suppose there were a mistake and Keith married as he had planned? Suppose my own scheme fell to pieces and he again escaped me? Here was the whole thing in my hands, and something for which I could never be blamed . . . I hanged him, and I do not regret it.

'None the less, I do fear that the law might not see the matter as I see it, as the merited act of a father correcting a fractious son. For that reason I am giving you this explanation, and I must also tell you that by the time you get to read it, after your return from work, I shall have gone on into the land where all evils are levelled and there is only the tranquility of the just . . .

'Ambrose.'

Maria laid the letter aside on the table.

'Crazy as a bed bug!' Pulp commented.

'Usually,' Maria said, 'I hand a dossier of the facts to the police for them to analyse — but in this instance I think

I would overplay my hand if I did so. I think the best thing would be for one of you here to go over to Mr. Robinson's place and upon getting no answer, call the police. Mr. Robinson's body will be found. There will be an inquest. Possibly his demise — his suicide — will be put down to grief at the loss of his son. I do not think there will be any other confession of guilt beyond that given in this letter. Clearly the man was insane — criminally so — and as such he was incapable of realizing it.'

'Does this mean you are not going to do anything to us?' Pat asked quickly.

'I am not the law, Pat,' Maria answered

'There remains the fact that I tried to finish you,' Gregory Taylor said quietly. 'I must have been crazy. I got that scared of what might happen — '

'I know: you were trying to protect your father.' Maria gave a final look about her and her gaze finally settled on Pulp. 'Mr. Martin, we are leaving forthwith,' she said abruptly. 'Come with me and you can carry my bags down to the car.'

We do hope that you have enjoyed reading this large print book.

Did you know that all of our titles are available for purchase?

We publish a wide range of high quality large print books including:
Romances, Mysteries, Classics
General Fiction
Non Fiction and Westerns

Special interest titles available in large print are:
The Little Oxford Dictionary
Music Book, Song Book
Hymn Book, Service Book

Also available from us courtesy of Oxford University Press:
Young Readers' Dictionary
(large print edition)
Young Readers' Thesaurus
(large print edition)

For further information or a free brochure, please contact us at:
Ulverscroft Large Print Books Ltd.,
The Green, Bradgate Road, Anstey,
Leicester, LE7 7FU, England.
Tel: (00 44) **0116 236 4325**
Fax: (00 44) **0116 234 0205**

A TIME FOR MURDER

John Glasby

Carlos Galecci, a top man in organized crime, has been murdered — and the manner of his death is extraordinary . . . He'd last been seen the previous night, entering his private vault, to which only he knew the combination. When he fails to emerge by the next morning, his staff have the metal door cut open — to discover Galecci dead with a knife in his back. Private detective Johnny Merak is hired to find the murderer and discover how the impossible crime was committed — but is soon under threat of death himself . . .